GU00458584

THE DUKE WHO DARED

ALL THAT GLITTERS

TAMMY ANDRESEN

SWIFT ROMANCE
PUBLISHING

Copyright © 2023 by Tammy Andresen

All rights reserved.

No part of this book may be reproduced in any form or by any electronic or mechanical means, including information storage and retrieval systems, without written permission from the author, except for the use of brief quotations in a book review.

❀ Created with Vellum

Keep up with all the latest news, sales, freebies, and releases by joining my newsletter!

www.tammyandresen.com

Hugs!

PROLOGUE

Miss Aubrey Fairfield lifted up her chin from the stitching she'd been hunched over when the bell on the door of her Cheapside shop rang with its usual light tinkle.

Had a customer forgot her pelisse? A parcel of her other purchases?

The door opened, allowing the damp evening air to filter into the warm interior, fanning Aubrey's neck.

She'd seen the last customer out and was just finishing a piece before she locked up for the evening.

But as she turned, the strange man in the doorway stopped her cold. "We're closed," she said, a tremor moving through her.

"We?" he asked with the sort of smile that made the hair rise on the back of her neck. His hat was pulled low, disguising his eyes, but his angular jaw and hard mouth were in clear view. "Don't be silly, Miss Fairfield. I know it's just you here."

Cold fear slid down her spine. Her shop was named Beauchamp's, after the former owner. But most thought she was Beauchamp, and she'd allowed them to do so because it helped hide her true identity. But this stranger already knew who she really was. Disconcerted, she rose from her chair. "I don't—"

He tsked, stopping her words. "Let's not waste time, shall we? I know that you are the daughter of the Marquess of Stallworth."

She swallowed hard. His bastard daughter. Not many knew these details. How did he?

"And I also know that once upon a time, the Rivermore Diamond belonged to you."

She drew in a trembling breath as she tried to step back. The blue diamond necklace had been sold by her mother years ago. The stone was Aubrey's one gift from her father, meant to act as a dowry for her, or perhaps just to provide for her future. She looked around her rented shop and rubbed her callused hands together.

"Then you know that I don't have it any longer." She lifted her chin and stared at him in an attempt to show courage, even if she was far from feeling it. Then she attempted to take a step back, but the table behind her stopped her progress.

The man gave her a wicked grin, his long, lanky frame moving with an easy yet sinister grace that stole her breath and made her tremble in fear as he moved closer. "Oh, but you can get it. Or should I say, we can get it."

She shook her head. "I can't. I don't have the faintest idea..."

"Lord Hampstead has it, bought for a fraction of its value and gifted to his late wife when he purchased it from your mother."

She scooted around the table, hoping to place some physical barrier between her and this man. "That has nothing to do with me. Please leave, I—"

"Not yet," he said as he reached into his pocket, another jolt of fear making her freeze. But it was only a large satchel that he drew from its depths. He tossed it on the table, where it landed with a hard, clinking *thump*. "We've still got a few points to discuss."

"Points?"

"See, no one will question Cecelia Fairfield's daughter purchasing the stone that once belonged to her."

This man wanted *her* to purchase the stone? She clasped her hands in front of her, attempting to reason her way out of whatever situation in which she'd managed to find herself tangled. "Perhaps. If anyone even knew that I was her daughter. Which they don't, as you well know."

He waved his hand. "That's the beauty of it. Perhaps no one will know. I'm sure you hope they don't. But if they ask…if someone is curious, starts to poke about, you won't seem strange in any way. The stone has a sentimental value to you, and it's only right that you'd want it back."

Her brow crinkled. What was this man talking about? It hardly made sense.

"You'll take this money, and you'll go to Lord Hampstead's auction and you'll purchase the stone."

Her jaw worked as her mind spun. Purchase the stone? "I'm not of their class. I have no escort. No right. No—"

He pulled out a sheet of paper from his other pocket and carefully unfolded it. "Hush now. We're discussing several key points. Remember? I've taken the liberty of purchasing your shop."

She looked at the paper, her chest so tight she could hardly breathe. At the bottom were two signatures, Beauchamp's and that of John Smith. "Mister Smith?"

"That's right," he said, pointing at the line where the shop was listed. "If you'd like to keep your business, you'll do as I say."

The trembling in her stomach worsened and she placed a hand over her belly. She barely survived now. If the shop were taken from her… "Please."

He gave a faint chuckle. "Now we're getting somewhere." Then he carefully folded the sheet again. "You're to take this money, six thousand pounds to be precise, and purchase the stone at the auction. Find a way. Whatever is left when you're done is yours to keep. At that time, I'll return and you'll give me the stone in exchange for this deed."

"You're going to give me the shop?"

"That's right, so don't fail." He reached across the table then, pulling the spectacles from her face. The brush of his fingers made her jolt back, his touch as frightening as the rest of him.

"Fake?" he asked. They were clear glass, not actually for vision but they helped her, along with her padded clothing, to hide in plain sight.

It was easier to be a tradeswoman without anyone knowing of her birth.

Bastards were not looked kindly upon and taking on a new identity had saved her from the torment she'd faced as a child—until now.

He crushed the spectacles in his hand and then dropped them on the table. The cold look in his eyes made her shrink back and she noted several cuts on his hand. He reached up and touched her face. Warm blood smeared across her skin. She jerked her head back at his touch but he only smiled wider. "Use your looks. A woman as beautiful as you can open any door she chooses."

"And if I do...fail?"

He leaned closer, the smile disappearing as a hard expression crossed his face. Then he patted the pocket that held the deed. "Don't." His hand reached out, clamping down in a hard grip that made her cry out. She tried to pull her hand away but he held it fast, crushing the fingers that she used to make her living. "I'd hate to tell all of London whose daughter you are and what a whore you had for a mother. How many ladies will come to your shop after that? Hmmm?" And then he let her hand go.

She pulled her arms close, wrapping them about her body as she eyed him warily.

She swallowed down a lump as he nudged the bag closer. "Mister Smith. Please. I've no resources to enact your plan. I can't attend, I'm sure they'd not allow a woman to bid."

His gaze slid down her. "I hear your mother was beautiful as well. Do you look like her?"

"What does it matter?"

"You ought to make Hampstead an offer he can't refuse. He's a lonely widower, you know."

For the first time since the man had arrived, something other than fear slid through her. White-hot anger. Aubrey knew exactly what he meant. He wanted her to give Hampstead her body in exchange for the diamond. She'd rather be dead than be used in such a way. Her mother had made a life of selling herself to the highest bidder and it was a choice that Aubrey had sworn she would never take.

THE DUKE WHO DARED

Not ever. Not for anyone, not even herself. "When is the auction?"

He shook his head, his eyes assessing her as he looked her up and down. She said a small prayer of thanks for the padded clothing that disguised her body from his gaze. "A week from tomorrow."

That didn't give her much time. "And who is to say that I won't just leave with your money?"

Quicker than she could breathe, he grabbed her hand, half pulling her onto the table. Her hip bit into the corner, a cry of pain erupting from her lips. His front pressed to her back, his hot breath in her ear. "You don't want to know," he said through clenched teeth.

He tightened his hand on her wrist, her fingers going numb as she gave another cry. He finally let her go.

"I'll be back after the auction. Don't fail, Miss Fairfield."

She pulled her arm close to her body, watching as he retreated from the shop, the bag of coins still sitting on the table.

Don't fail? How would she ever succeed?

CHAPTER ONE

NICHOLAS HART, the Duke of Wingate, was a devil of a man.

Aubrey stood half hidden behind the fronds of a fern as the duke completely blocked her view of the rest of the ballroom.

Why him? And why now? She had a mission to complete. Instead, she watched as he whispered conspiratorially in some debutante's ear. The woman laughed as though he had just uttered the funniest, most interesting tidbit in the entire world.

Fool.

Why were some women so determined to ruin themselves?

Then again, Aubrey was far more concerned about her own future than that of some debutante. Quick inquiries into the auction had yielded distressing news...she could not attend without a benefactor, of which she had none.

Her best friend and client, Miss Emily Cranston, had come up with the only viable idea. Ask the Marquess of Stallworth, Aubrey's absent father, to escort her to the auction.

She hated the notion of asking him for anything, nearly as much as she hated the idea of seeing Nick Hart again. But there wasn't really another option. Stallworth had given her the stone to provide for her future, she needed his help, this one time, to provide for herself again.

Surely the marquess would not deny her this one favor? But she had to find the man first, and currently, one very large obstacle stood in her way—Nick.

She gave an indelicate snort as she stared at Nick's dark, wavy hair and piercing green eyes. Like the grass in Ireland, she'd once murmured to him in a moment of weakness.

She'd never even been to Ireland. She'd just heard the Irish woman who worked for the milliner in the small village she'd lived in with her mother as a child say the same. And she'd repeated the words to Nick like the silly girl she'd been.

He'd given her that charming half smile of his, the one where he only quirked one side of his mouth, and then he'd winked. "I know, Ducky."

Even at fourteen, he'd been full of himself. And by fifteen, several ladies in the village had been full of him too. Aubrey had even caught him on one occasion with the dairy maid. Nothing wilted a crush faster than watching the boy she'd adored for years make the maid squeal with delight.

She shook her head. That didn't matter now.

He'd never even known she was alive back then. All coltish legs and untamed hair, she hadn't been much to look at when she was twelve. Her cheeks had been too prominent, her eyes too big, her gait awkward as she tried to catch up to her growing body.

She'd not been anything that Nick had been interested in pursuing. And several of his local friends had taken it upon themselves to torture her with her obvious crush and her unfortunate birth. Nick had tolerated her mostly, but the others…

Nick's two best friends, Jacob Robinson, a baron's son, and Eric Henderson, a viscount's heir, had taken it upon themselves to prove to her that she did not belong anywhere near Nick. Until she'd seen him with the maid, then she'd finally stopped trying to spend time with him.

She'd done as her mother had asked and taken up an apprenticeship as a dressmaker. Despite the fact that her mother was a lady and her father a marquess, she'd not been born in wedlock and her one fallback, the stone, had been sold before Aubrey had been old enough to object.

So she'd taken the apprenticeship and moved to London to train as a seamstress and dressmaker. And Nick had likely forgotten she ever existed. But she had not forgotten him...

Always handsome, Nick was rich, popular, titled. He'd never had to fight for anything. Never had to work a day in his life. Never had to know how it felt to be told he was ugly or unwanted.

And he'd certainly never been blackmailed into purchasing a diamond. Never had to know what it meant to fight to claim a tiny corner of the world just as she was doing now.

Which only added to her irritation, because right this moment, he stood directly between her and her only way forward—her father.

And for some maddening reason, when Nick had come near her hiding spot in the ballroom, he'd stayed, catching the attention of the annoying little giggly twit who currently batted her eyelashes up at him.

The other woman nodded and then, much to Aubrey's chagrin, looked at Aubrey with a slight frown.

Aubrey straightened. Why would that woman look at her? What had just been said?

And then her mouth set in a hard line. Because the simpering debutante with her pouty lips and her swaying hips began sauntering toward Aubrey.

Vaguely, she recognized the young woman, her mother having brought her into Aubrey's shop for several gowns, but Aubrey had not made the flowing silk gown the other woman currently wore. A small favor now, though Aubrey noted that the work was not nearly as well crafted. The embroidery was not as fine, the sleeves not as artfully arranged.

The woman stopped in front of her, her gaze assessing as she searched Aubrey's face. Some light of recognition lit her eyes as she studied Aubrey's face. "I know you from somewhere."

Aubrey let out a small sigh of annoyance. "Yes," she said.

Her disguise, which she did not wear tonight, normally hid her curves. And this evening, she'd gone without the glasses, severe hair style, and padded clothes to make certain no one recognized her from her shop. She did not want clients to realize she was at this event.

But still, she couldn't hide the blue of her eyes, or the color of her hair, or the curve of her mouth. Did this lady recognize her?

She glanced down at the dress she'd sewn herself, which hugged her body, clinging to every curve. Her hair was swept back, pinned into large curls, and she'd allowed a few to artfully escape about her face. She'd tried to appear the debutante tonight and she'd hardly recognized herself. But this woman still noted something familiar in Aubrey's appearance.

Did Nick also know who she was? Aubrey looked far different than she had as a young lady. In fact, many declared her a beauty now. She had grown into her legs, and her face had taken on a less harsh symmetry. Her cheekbones no longer protruded from her face, they now looked classically shaped. And her eyes weren't too big, like they'd been before, but were now just the sort of doe eyes to which men seemed drawn.

Not that she wanted any man's attention. She didn't intend to marry after she'd worked so hard to support herself. Nor did she wish to take a lover. There was too much risk of pregnancy and she'd not subject a child to the life she'd had as an outcast.

Her only goal was to recapture the lost Rivermore Diamond for Mr. Smith so that she could keep her shop and go back to her quiet life where she managed to hide in plain sight. Odd, but she was more comfortable hidden in her padded dresses than she was tonight. She felt exposed with the gown that hugged her curves and showed her decolletage.

But she'd needed to look her part this evening. She was the daughter of a marquess, after all. And she was here tonight to ask for his help, a fact that she hated. But there was nothing to be done for it. She needed an escort to the auction where the stone was being sold, and she'd not allow another man who might want some other kind of payment for his efforts.

If only her mother hadn't declared her too homely to marry and then sold the stone when she was twelve.

Her fist clenched as she pushed her anger at her mother aside.

"Where do I know you from?" The woman's comment drew Aubrey back to the present.

Aubrey didn't wish to say *I'm one of your seamstresses.* She wasn't meant to be here at this ball. She'd been hiding in this corner for a reason.

Pasting a smile on her face, she recalled a ball from several weeks prior. She knew them all from her customers. "Did we meet at the Winchester soirée?"

Confusion knitted the other woman's brow. "Of course. That must be it."

She nodded. "Pleasure to see you again, Lady Rebecca."

"And you." She didn't need to address Aubrey further as Aubrey's address already proved that Rebecca was of the greater rank.

"Can I assist you in some way?"

The other woman's entire demeanor changed as the simpering smile pulled at her lips. "I believe you can."

That made Aubrey's brow knit as the other woman threaded her arm through Aubrey's. "How?" Aubrey asked as she looked down at the other woman, who had to be four or five inches shorter than Aubrey.

Lady Rebecca's smile grew. "He wishes to speak with you, and I wish for him to escort me to the theater on Friday, so…"

Aubrey's lips pursed. She knew very well who the *he* they spoke of was. What she didn't know was why he would wish to discuss anything with her? And why had he sent Lady Rebecca to fetch Aubrey? Why not just come over to her if he wanted to converse?

But Rebecca answered that question for her. "If anyone asks, we're great friends, which is why I made the introduction."

Of course. She should have known that a duke could only speak to a lady by way of introduction.

Though Aubrey had never attended an event like this, she had overheard enough in her shop and learned plenty about how to behave at one from her mother, who had apparently been the belle of the ball until she been ruined by the marquess.

As a young man, her father had been quite the rake, and her mother had fallen neatly into his clutches. Did he regret the affair? Her birth? He must...

But she had another lord to attend to at this exact moment. She angled her chin higher as they approached the duke. He was a part of her past she didn't wish to revisit, and what was more, she had a mission here and she would not be distracted.

Emily had gotten her this invitation by claiming that Aubrey was a distant cousin from the country come to stay. A farce that Emily had managed to slip past her mother at great personal risk and not one Aubrey was likely to make again.

"Hello," Nick said, his baritone far deeper now, though she caught a hint of the boy that had turned all man. His green eyes penetrated deep into her soul as her breath caught at meeting them again. Damn her foolish body and its reaction to him. How could he still, after all this time, evoke this sort of feeling?

She gave her head the slightest incline. "Your Grace."

"You told her who I was," he said, clearly talking to Rebecca, his voice colored by just a touch of displeasure. But his comment indicated that he hadn't wished for her to know his identity. Did that mean that he didn't know hers? It must.

"I did not." Rebecca's tongue clucked. "I kept my end of the bargain, and you'll keep yours."

Aubrey's brows shot up. Perhaps Rebecca was not as empty-headed as Aubrey had assumed. She and Nick had clearly made a bargain of sorts. "Why," Aubrey asked, now too curious to hold her tongue, "would you introduce another woman to a man you wished to escort you?"

"Oh, she doesn't want me," Nick answered. "She's got her sights set on far more respectable prey. I'm just a means to an end."

Aubrey looked at Rebecca, whose grimace confirmed the truth of his statement. A woman who didn't want Nick? Interesting.

But not compelling enough to distract her. Or at least, she'd pretend that he wasn't dizzyingly handsome long enough to escape back to her corner and keep searching for the marquess. She knew that he was older, that he wore a red vest, and that he had a large moustache. Those were all the details Emily had given her before she'd been whisked away for her first dance.

"Well, if that is all…" Rebecca took a step back. "I'll see you on Friday, Your Grace." And then the other woman turned and disappeared into the crowd, leaving her with Nick. Her spine stiffened.

"Alone at last," he murmured, moving a bit closer.

And despite the shiver of awareness that spread through her, she took a half step back. "We are in a large crowd. That is hardly alone."

His brows lifted as a devilish smile, one she recognized, quirked one side of his mouth. "Yes, but no one else is here in this conversation."

"Not even me," she quipped, taking another step away from him, though her path was blocked by two elderly matrons with large plumes of feathers coming out of their headdresses. She had to stop for a moment and Nick took advantage by stepping in front of her.

"We've only just begun to converse. Why leave?"

"Because." She scooted to the side, the matrons finally passing them by, but he matched her move, blocking her exit once again. "As I've stated, I've no interest in speaking to you."

"Many women find me quite charming."

How disappointingly familiar. She stopped, her chin snapping up. "Well, perhaps you should find one of them to converse with."

"But I wish to speak with you," he answered, giving her that confident smile once again that completely rattled her composure.

"The arrogance you display is beyond irritating. Would you please excuse me?"

"But I'm curious about you." His gaze narrowed as he seemed to study her once again.

She nearly rolled her eyes. Did he really think that he could just accost her and monopolize her entire evening to satisfy his curiosity? *Dukes.*

"The feeling is not mutual," she said as she attempted to turn. And that's when she saw him—the Marquess of Stallworth. A man of advanced years, he had on a red cravat and sported a large moustache, the sort that covered his entire mouth. But more importantly, she'd recognize his blue eyes anywhere. They were the same color and shape as her own.

Aubrey pivoted, intent upon putting herself directly in her father's path, when a hand shot out and touched her arm.

Sparks of awareness heated her skin as her chin snapped up, her gaze meeting his once again. "Your Grace."

"Don't leave yet," he rumbled, moving closer. "I…"

But his voice trailed off. For a moment she forgot she hated him, forgot she was here to see someone else. She began to drown in the green of his gaze, the strong jaw, the full lips.

She shook her head. "Let me go."

"Of course," he answered, removing his hand. "I only meant to…"

But she stopped listening as her head snapped to the side. Nick had done it. He'd distracted her and now she had lost sight of the marquess. Searching, she craned her neck to try to spot him, but she could not find the man anywhere. A small cry fell from her lips. She'd lost the man she'd come to meet.

Without another word to the duke, she turned on her heel and started across the room. She had to find Stallworth and forget that Nick ever existed.

CHAPTER TWO

SHE WAS GETTING AWAY.

Nick didn't even know her name. Somehow, he'd not gotten to that part yet. He tried to search back in his mind and figure out where he'd gone wrong. Normally, he was as smooth as freshly churned butter.

Perhaps he was out of practice. It had been some time since he'd even attempted to lure a woman into his bed.

He'd grown so bored with the entire process. Of course, it was entertaining to find a new woman, seduce her, but then...

He had to do the inevitable parting of ways and while some women took it well, others...did not.

But even with that, he was just tired of his life. The endless parties, the drinking, the women, the parade of bad behavior that left him feeling a little lower each morning when he finally woke from a stupor.

His father was dead, after all, trivial bad behavior was unlikely to punish the old duke, and if Nick no longer enjoyed the process either...

So he'd largely quit the entire life. He went to his boxing club, balanced his accounts, rode in the park, went to bed at a reasonable hour. It wasn't the solution, he knew that. It filled him with a different sort of restlessness, but his gut told him that he needed to continue this way until he found the answer to a question that resurfaced again and again. What did he do with the rest of his life?

He still fully intended to punish his late father. The old man deserved nothing less. Which meant that he'd not marry, not have an heir, allow the title to go to his second cousin Herbert. It was a large gift to give a man he didn't like or respect, but he didn't know what else to do.

He'd not marry one of the glittering ladies currently floating about the floor. Not only was that his father's dearest wish, it would surely mean more of the same.

And while celibacy sounded dreadful, he'd been more or less content with his life until tonight.

First, he'd come here because Lady Wittcoff, the hostess of this party, was his former lover. Wanting a good turnout and knowing that a previously rakish duke-turned-recluse would bring every guest, she'd insisted that he come. And by insist, he meant that she'd threatened to release specific information about his past activities should he not come.

He sighed. Part of him had wanted to allow her to do so. He didn't really care what others thought, nor did he like being threatened, but in the end, he'd decided to come because... He drew in a ragged breath. Because he was turning over some new leaf, and dredging up the past seemed ill-advised.

Which was ridiculous. He didn't want to marry and he was a duke. If he changed his mind, he could have any woman he wished.

Except for the one currently stalking away from him.

Her indifference made her all the more intriguing. He'd been enchanted from the first glance. Tall yet curvy, her blonde hair thick, lush, and barely contained by the pins holding it back, she had high cheekbones, full lips, and the sort of eyes a man could fall into like a crystal-clear pool of blue water.

He sucked in a breath as he started after her, watching the sway of her hips as she hurried away.

Where was she going? And what sort of woman dismissed a duke? One he wished to know more about.

He watched her moving across the floor, her eyes trained in one direction. He followed her stare and squinted. Was that Stallworth she watched? Why would a young, vibrant debutante want anything to do with Stallworth?

She caught the notice of several men who stood in the crowded room, their eyes following his mystery woman's progress across the floor.

His jaw clenched as he glared at each in turn, telling them with his eyes to stay in their position. While Lady Wittcoff and several other women might be able to lead him about, no man would. Of that he was certain.

He made steady progress catching up to his goddess as Stallworth moved toward the exit of the room. When he exited, the lady in question stopped, her shoulders dropping.

His brows lifted as he took advantage of her pause to catch up to her.

"Miss," he rumbled as stopped just a foot behind her. "I must insist."

She turned, glaring at him. "Insist? What right do you have to do so?"

His lips parted as he noted the irritation that laced her voice. It bordered on vitriol. Had they been lovers already? She sounded like a woman he'd wronged, but he'd remember her if they had been. There was little chance he'd forget a face like hers. Her beauty was unparalleled.

He drank her in for a moment...her high cheekbones, the slender column of her neck, the delicate arch of her brows, but he resisted the urge to reach for her again.

"I don't even know your name."

She let out a long breath as her brows drew together. "You don't?"

He would surely have remembered this woman if they'd been together, but the question made him once again think that they'd known each other before. "I'm afraid I don't. Should I?"

17

Slowly her face relaxed into a neutral, unreadable expression. "No. You shouldn't. Now, if you'll excuse me." She turned, clearly intent upon leaving him standing once again.

"Wait."

He saw her hesitate, and in that moment, he took advantage, moving closer. He ought to ask her name, anything to know more about her, but once again, he forgot all the rehearsed maneuvers he knew for how to pursue a woman.

"Why are you following the Marquess of Stallworth?"

She spun about again, her mouth dropping open. "Why would you ask that?"

He arched one brow, his arms crossing again. He could tell by her reaction he'd been correct. "Don't deny it."

"I'm not. I just…" Then she trailed off. "It's none of your business."

Something about her brought out a well of feelings that he hadn't experienced in years. He felt more like himself— No. That wasn't right. He felt interested and alive. "It is if I make it."

She snorted then. A full-on snort that was at complete odds with her beauty and every woman around her. For some reason, it made him wish to throw his head back and laugh.

"You don't believe me?" he asked.

"I don't care," she retorted. "You can go to the devil."

He moved closer, so close that their chests almost touched. He caught a whiff of her scent, like gardenias and roses, and took a deep inhale. Delightful.

"I just might. But perhaps I should take you with me." The repartee had his blood roaring in his veins.

Her jaw hardened as her chin notched harder. "You wouldn't dare."

"Oh, princess." He didn't know what else to call her. "You seem to know me well enough to know that I would and I will."

Her eyes widened and something sparked inside him. A familiarity that he couldn't quite place, but there was an existing intimacy between them. It was undeniable. "I need to go," she whispered.

"No you don't," he said as he reached for her waist. He was the worst sort of cad but in this moment, he couldn't let her leave again. They were circling about something and he had no idea what.

"Let me go, Nick, or I shall—"

"Nick?" he asked, pulling her closer. That's when he noted the crowd. The one that circled them but also had backed up to give them room. *Shite.* He eased back, knowing full well that he was making a scene.

And she took full advantage.

Slipping from his grasp, she started across the room again, lifting her skirts as she fled. So...she thought to get away, did she?

He followed again, this time at a more leisurely pace.

If she wanted a chase, he'd give her a good one. That was one promise he could make.

———

AUBREY SLIPPED OUT into the darkness, breathing a sigh of relief. She'd finally managed to escape from the duke, though it hadn't been easy to lose him in the crowd, collect her pelisse, and leave.

Worse still, she'd missed the marquess. By the time she'd made it out of the ballroom, he was gone, exiting the ball and heading down the stairs toward his carriage.

It had made her fists ball in anger and fear. She had no idea how likely he was to have helped her, but he'd been her one hope. And this had been her opportunity to finally meet the man who'd sired and then abandoned her. Aubrey's mother had been dreadful, but at least she'd participated in her life.

And then there was Mr. Smith. What would he do to her if she failed? Tension coiled inside her once again, afraid to know. He'd purchased her shop and threatened to close her business. That was bad enough, but what if he meant worse? The memory of his touch made her shoulders curl in as she shivered.

"Aubrey," Emily called from the top of the stairs. "You're leaving?"

She turned and went back up the stairs to her friend. "Stallworth is gone. There is no reason for me to stay."

"Did you…were you able to talk with him?"

Aubrey shook her head. "No."

"Are you disappointed?"

"Not really." They both knew that Aubrey was telling a partial truth at best. No matter how many times she told herself she wanted no man in her life, there was a part of her that was curious about the man who'd sired her.

Emily nodded, her slender shoulders drooping as a single strand of her dark, silky hair fell from her neatly pinned coif. A delicate beauty, she was as kind as she was attractive. "I'm still not certain why you suddenly want this diamond?"

Aubrey grimaced as she turned her face away from her friend. She didn't wish to burden Emily with the story of Mr. Smith. Emily had her own issues. "I'm just attempting to reconcile my past. That's all."

"It's a shame you weren't able to speak with him. I know he'd help you if you asked." She sighed. "Perhaps my father could take you to the auction."

Aubrey shook her head. She'd not put the baron in such a compromising position. Attending the auction with him would surely spark rumor and Emily's mother would never agree to such a favor. "That's all right. I'll find another way."

"My brother? I can write to him."

Aubrey held up a hand. "You are too kind, my dear friend."

Emily winced. "I'm sorry that I couldn't help you more tonight. My mother saw that my dance card was full and…" Emily winced.

"I understand." Aubrey reached out and squeezed her friend's hand. Emily had already done more than Aubrey should ever ask. "Thank you for trying. You are the very best friend."

Emily wrapped her arms about Aubrey's shoulders. "I have to go back inside, but put on your pelisse. The spring air still has a chill about it."

"I will," Aubrey replied, hugging her friend back. "Go, before your mother notices your absence."

Emily nodded into her shoulder before she pulled away. "Be safe. I'll keep thinking of another way to help you."

Aubrey didn't answer as her friend rushed away. Aubrey hadn't told Emily about the deal she'd struck with Mr. Smith. A woman like Emily would only worry to know, and besides, Emily would never understand what it meant to have to care for one's self.

Aubrey had to take a few risks to secure her future. Didn't she?

She drew in a steadying breath as she retraced her steps down the stairs and started along the cobblestone street, intent upon finding a hack.

But a voice stopped her cold.

"What auction?"

Nick. Her eyes closed for a moment and then opened, though she didn't turn around. She hadn't lost him after all. "That's none of your concern."

"Really? But it is the concern of the Marquess of Stallworth?"

She balled her hands into her pelisse. "That's also not your concern."

"He's a letch. You shouldn't be anywhere near him." Nick moved closer with every word, she could hear his footsteps as his voice grew louder. Her pulsed thrummed to the strike of his steps.

"First of all, you can hardly throw such stones. You have a reputation of your own," she answered as he moved close enough that she could feel the heat of his skin. She sucked in a breath.

He let out a growl of dissent, though she knew the words to be true. What was more, she was certain she was far safer in the marquess's company than she was with Nick. "But I would never—"

She spun then, her shoulder bumping his chest as she faced him, her chin notching up. "You would. You approached me specifically for lecherous purposes. Don't deny it." A muscle in the back of his jaw jumped, though he did not say a word. Pointing a finger into his chest, she continued. "Well, let me be clear, I'm not interested in what you're offering."

"I didn't offer anything."

She rolled her eyes then. Slowly and deliberately. "I'm not some silly, foolish debutante. I know what you're after."

He dropped his face lower until his breath fanned her cheeks and her breath stalled in her chest. "What are you, then, if not silly or foolish?"

His question was so low and deep that it rolled through her like a wave of water, washing over every square inch of her body. "I'm nothing," she whispered back, her voice catching as the words left her mouth. She shouldn't have told him that.

For him to know any of the specifics of her life was to put herself at his mercy.

But he straightened away, his gaze narrowing. "Oh, you're most certainly something."

CHAPTER THREE

WITH EVERY MOMENT that Nick spent with this woman, he became more curious. What was her past, her present, what did she seek for a future, and what sort of man did she like, if not him?

He felt as though he were coming back to wakefulness after a long sleep. Years and years of sleep.

It was not just the sizzle of attraction, it was the challenge that she offered. No, that wasn't right either. She seemed like she might be in trouble, and something rumbled through him to protect her.

Which was ridiculous. He knew nothing about her. And even less about the sort of trouble in which she might find herself. It was a mistake to get involved, but he wanted to insert himself anyway. "Why don't you tell me what's wrong?"

"No," came her single word answer. "Your Grace." Her hand came to his chest, her palm lying flat on his jacket, clearly meant to put distance between them, but heat flared from her touch. "It's best if you just leave me be."

His brows arched. His head was telling him the same thing. And she'd walked away from him twice. "Let's start with names, shall we? You know mine…"

Her hand dropped and she took a large step back. "No."

No? They must have known each other for her to be so resistant. "You're upset I've forgotten you."

A flush rose in her cheeks as anger sparked in her eyes. Blast, but she was glorious when she was irritated. "Apparently, I was utterly forgettable."

So they had known each other! He straightened his shoulders as he looked down at her. "I doubt that very much. More likely, I was a complete cad."

The air rushed from her lips as uncertainty flashed in her eyes. Finally, he'd cracked her defenses. A rush of victory coursed through him.

"That too," she whispered. "But either way, I know better than to share my problems with you."

His teeth clenched. "Is that so?" But some truth rang in his ears, making him ache a bit. His parents had never been people he could count on. Not really. They'd each led their own lives, separate from him and apart from one another. He was a necessity to the dukedom, nothing more, and they'd left him to be raised by a series of nannies and tutors.

And he'd acted much the same his entire adult life. He kept everyone at a distance. Always. But that realization gave him a tiny window into where he wished to go, an answer to one of the questions for which he'd been searching.

Despite being certain he'd never marry, never live through the hell of marriage, he could now see that one of the things he needed was to make an actual connection with someone.

The realization made his head snap back. How had it taken all this time to figure that out?

And why had this woman so effortlessly brought out the realization? "Why don't you try sharing your problems and see what happens?"

She shook her head. "I don't..."

He lifted his hand up then. Rather than grab her again, he lightly touched his fingertips to her cheek. "What auction?"

Her eyes fluttered closed. "Lord Hampstead is hosting a private auction in five days' time."

"An auction? Of what?" He furrowed his brow, curious where this was going.

"Jewelry. Some of the pieces he'd collected for his late wife. Financial troubles, I hear."

He cocked his head to the side, assessing her. "You want to go to a jewelry auction?"

"Yes."

"For the purpose of?"

"Buying one of the pieces, of course. What else?"

His mouth opened and then closed. Did he ask why she wished to buy gems for herself? What of her father, brother, husband? He'd assumed that she was a debutante the way she'd hidden herself in the corner, but perhaps she wasn't. "And you have no one to buy it for you?"

Her eyes snapped with irritation then. "I can buy it myself."

He studied her for several seconds. He'd realized that while some of her irritation was directed at him, he might not be the only man she didn't like or appreciate. The thought gave him a small bit of solace. "I'm sure you can."

But that only made her shoulders sink again. "No. You're right. I can't. I'm not allowed into the auction without an escort, of which I have none."

He stopped. "You need an escort?"

"Yes," she answered, her chin sinking as she looked at the ground. "Preferably one who does not require me to compromise my values in order to bring me to the event that will allow me to buy back my birthright."

He was beginning to understand. "Why would the marquess be a good choice for that?"

"Why not him?"

Nick shook his head. "Trust me when I say he is not the man to ask if you're not willing to pay for his help with…" He stopped, not wanting to say that she'd have to enter the man's bed.

Her gaze snapped back up to his. "I highly doubt that would be the arrangement."

Perhaps not. But he'd seen Emily and she'd certainly been an innocent. She likely just didn't understand. "Let me help you."

"No."

There was that word again. "What if I swear on my title that I'll not lay a finger on you?"

Her gaze narrowed. "Why would you do that?"

"I'm not entirely certain." He shook his head. "But I can tell you, it's almost as important for me as it is for you."

He saw her hesitation. She was tempted. She caught her lip between her teeth, and another memory tugged at him. He wanted to reach out and touch her cheek again. He started to lift his hand but then she shook her head. "I just don't think I should."

And then she turned and fled into the night. He considered chasing her for a moment but he'd laid chase enough for one evening.

Besides. He knew precisely who to ask to discover more about her…Miss Emily Cranston. And he was certain Emily's mother would give him the audience he needed.

———

THE NEXT DAY, Aubrey attempted to attend the words of her customer.

"I feel as though chartreuse brings out the right hues in my skin," the woman continued. "And for the cut…"

Aubrey mumbled an unintelligible response, but her mind seemed unable to focus. She'd hardly slept the night before.

Between her missed opportunity with the marquess and Nick's insistent pursuit, her mind had been too busy.

Should she have trusted him? He was a rake, he'd made her feel small and worthless as a girl, but he'd never hurt her.

In fact, he'd been nicer to her than most. He'd spent time with her, at least until he'd discovered other girls and they'd discovered him too…

She sighed. But he also brought out so many feelings that she didn't wish to revisit. The feeling of being less, of being unwanted and ugly. Of being inferior.

It was these very feelings she hoped to escape with the purchase of the diamond. If Mr. Smith kept his promise and gave her the deed to her shop, she could live her life on her terms and no one else's.

And somehow, it offended her sensibilities that she'd be lumped into the mass of women that had been linked with Nick. Even if he promised to keep his hands to himself, others would think she was his mistress.

Then she sighed. What did it matter? She'd have what she sought and she shuddered to think of what would happen if she wasn't able to attend the auction…if she didn't get the diamond. She'd lose her shop and be further from her dream than ever.

She stared unseeing at the green gown, lost in her own thoughts.

"You don't like peacock feathers?" her client asked, and Aubrey realized she'd hardly been listening.

"Oh no, not at all." Then she realized what she'd just said. "That is to say, I like them a great deal. Apologies. They'll be perfect with the color of this gown."

The woman gave her a long, narrow-eyed glare before she finally continued with her lengthy monologue about accessories. Aubrey gently patted the tight coif she'd fashioned low on her head.

She nearly sighed again as she pinned the dress into place and then began removing the gown to sew later.

The rest of the day passed much the same and it was with relief that she saw the last client out the door.

But her relief was short-lived. She had no more closed the wooden frame when the bell rang again to signal that the door had opened. Had she not locked it?

"Madame Beauchamp?" Nick asked, his deep voice rumbling straight through her as she spun about to face him. The color drained from her face and she pushed her glasses up further, as if they'd hide her identity.

They didn't. His eyes lit with recognition.

27

Aubrey swallowed down a lump. "How did you find me?"

He closed the door behind him, snapping the lock into place. "It doesn't matter."

"Unlock that door at once," she huffed as she started toward him. "What will people think?"

"No one saw me and besides, even if they did, they'll think I'm here buying a gift for my latest paramour."

That halted her steps. "All right, then. Answer my first question."

"Miss Cranston told me," he said with that rakish grin he wore so well.

She shook her head, not willing to believe his words. "Emily wouldn't."

"She did just tell me. Likely, because I told her that I had every intention of helping you." He glanced about the shop. "Nice place."

Her lips parted as she stared at him, not quite believing they were having this conversation. "Thank you."

"So you're a businesswoman?"

She winced. If he thought her a debutante, she had a certain matter of protection against any of his advances in the threat of privileged male relatives. Knowing the truth made this man even more dangerous. "As you can see, I'm not of your class."

"What does that have to do with anything?"

She supposed he was right. "You made promises. Do they still apply?"

"Of course." His eyes caught hers, holding her gaze in a way that both comforted and excited.

"You don't give up easily, do you?" she said as she finally broke their gaze, looking down at her work table.

"Nope. Endearing, isn't it?" He gave her a wicked grin as he leaned against the counter.

"Not really. Why are you here?"

He gave her a sidelong glance before he answered. "As I told Emily, to help you."

She shook her head. "Very few men, and even fewer lords, help a woman like me out of the goodness of their hearts."

A slight grimace pulled at his features. "True."

"And as we've discussed, I know you, so I am certain you're not the exception to the rule."

He straightened. "How do we know each other, precisely?" His gaze slid down her frame, her disguise hiding much of her figure. So why did his eyes make her feel exposed?

And why did part of her wish that he remembered her? She'd been hurt that he hadn't known who she was, if she were being honest, but it was bad enough that he knew what she looked like under the padding. Aubrey had no intention of reminding him that she was the girl who'd fawned over him as a child. The one who his friends had teased mercilessly. "If you don't remember, I'm not going to tell you."

He let out a long breath. "The old me was a real pain in the ass."

The old him? Had he changed? Her hands pressed to her stomach as she looked away. She'd not be lulled into trusting him. She didn't trust any man, but she knew with absolute certainty that she should not trust Nick. "You're different now?"

"I don't know," he answered with a shrug. "Trying to be. And I know when a woman needs assistance. And I already told you, for selfish reasons, it seems important that I help you."

Her breath trembled through her lips. Now that she could believe. Besides, she'd not met the marquess last night. She had four days until the auction and here was a chance to complete the task Mr. Smith had given her. Was she being foolish now not accepting his help? Who was she more afraid of? The duke or the mysterious man who'd threatened her? It was a difficult choice.

She didn't know how dastardly Mr. Smith's intentions were but she knew precisely what the man before her wanted... "I can't accept your help, Your Grace."

"Nick. You've used my given name already. Now, Aubrey—"

"Stop." Her name on his lips jolted her. First, because he'd discovered her given name and he still didn't remember her. How did he know it? "Who told you my name?"

His brow crinkled as though he were trying to puzzle out who she was.

"Emily did, of course."

Pain lanced through her. She'd meant nothing to him back then and that somehow hurt as much as the pain he and his friends had caused her. "I don't want to hear any more."

"But—"

She pulled up straighter. "You should leave."

CHAPTER FOUR

THE HELL he was going anywhere.

He straightened too. "Why don't you tell me what I did that has made you so angry?"

He could guess. Had they had an affair? Had he left her? Shame washed over him.

Then another thought hit him. Did she have a child? Was it his? He usually took great pains to see that he didn't impregnate a woman. He intended never to have a child. But she was exceptionally beautiful and he must have been dead drunk to not remember her.

"It doesn't matter now," she pushed out through gritted teeth. "I want you to leave."

"Boy or girl?" he asked, his gaze narrowing.

"What are you talking about?" She stopped, fully facing him.

"A child. Did we have a child?" The shame building in his chest throbbed painfully. He despised his parents for their neglect. They'd nearly killed him with indifference, but had he been any better?

"Don't be ridiculous," she scoffed, her nose wrinkling. "I'd never let you touch me."

His chest relaxed. "Good," he said as he combed a hand through his hair. But then he stopped midway through the gesture. "If I haven't touched you, then we didn't sleep together either?"

"Of course not," she said, and then her hands landed on her hips, her chin notching up.

Something sparked in him again. The stance, the shape of the chin, the fire in her eyes.

A memory rose up. A girl with a mass of untamed blonde hair and the spirit of an unbroken colt. All fire and a bit awkward, she'd followed him about the village near his father's country estate. "Ducky?"

The blood drained from her face. "Don't call me that," she whispered, pain lacing her voice.

He blinked several times. "Lucifer's left tit," he mumbled as he looked her up and down again. She was wearing some ridiculous costume now, her body lost in it, but he remembered her curves in that dress from the night before. The awkward girl had developed into a rare beauty. The ugly duckling turned beautiful swan.

Her eyes were still flashing and she wrenched off the glasses to give him an epic glare, the sort that might wilt a lesser man.

It was Ducky all right. Aubrey. Her mother had lived in a cottage in the village, gifted to her by his father. He knew it to be true, he'd happened upon the documents himself. Her mother, the daughter of an earl, had been unceremoniously tossed from her family when she'd had an illicit affair before marriage.

Aubrey was every bit the beauty her mother, Lady Cecelia, had been, but unlike her mother, a spirit of independence radiated from Aubrey in an incredibly attractive way. Her mother had been...

He sighed. Even as a boy he'd noticed Lady Cecelia's cloying techniques. His father must have fallen for them at some point. His parents had lived separate lives from each other and apparently their affairs had been the talk of London for years.

Was Stallworth her father? Is that why she sought him out? Because it was clear to him that Aubrey was not looking for a benefactor beyond helping her attend a single auction. She had a thriving business here, he'd seen it this afternoon. "I didn't mean to offend."

"You offended me long before now, and as long as we're acquainted, I'm sure you'll do it again. Which is why it would be best if you leave."

He grimaced, knowing that she did not like him. He might as well ask a few more uncomfortable questions. "Do you have motives for seeking out Stallworth beyond his aid at the auction?"

Her brow furrowed. "You already asked me that and I told you, Emily said that he would make a good escort—"

"Emily is wrong," he answered. "Unless he knows that you are Cecelia's daughter. Did you intend to tell him that?"

"How did you..."

Christ. He was in it now. "You've got his eyes."

Her cheeks went from pale to bright red, blood flushing them. "For a man who didn't know who I was five minutes ago, you're making a great many connections."

"Apologies for my intrusion. But even knowing of your relationship, I still maintain you should stay clear of the man. He brings nothing but destruction to everything he touches. I've seen it time and again."

She shook her head, her hand brushing over her eyes. "My own experiences supported your claim but I have to attend the auction. There is no other choice."

"If you tell him who you are, he might reject you from the first. If you don't, he'll likely proposition you and—"

She swayed then, her hand coming to her brow, and he stepped forward, his hands wrapping about her waist as he tucked her against his chest. "It's all right."

"It's not all right," she whispered. "How did that not occur to me sooner? He ruined an earl's daughter and then didn't marry her."

Nick could hardly answer. Her body molded to his, her lush breasts pressed to his chest, her flat belly pressing into his hips, her thighs resting against his. If it weren't for that damnable padding, he'd be able to feel even more of her. He longed to trace the ample curve of her hip, feel her behind, mold it with his hands.

He'd been too long without a woman, or she was perfect for him, because no female had ever felt this good in his arms.

His fingers spread out on her back as he settled her just a bit closer. "Either way, don't see him unless you're ready for all the answers."

She shook her head. "I just wanted to go to that auction. Why is my entire past being dredged up?"

"I don't know," he answered as he lightly traced her spine. "But my offer stands. I'll take you if you need. You can approach Stallworth separately when and if you're ready. Or not."

He felt her weaken against him, sinking further into his body. Her chin notched up, her eyes searching his, looking vulnerable for the first time. How could he have ever dismissed her as a girl? He should have seen the woman she'd become.

Her lips parted and then pressed together, her hands reaching for his biceps. The fact that she held him too made him swell with satisfaction, as though he'd achieved some major victory.

And then, slowly, she gave a nod. "I accept."

He smiled, one side of his mouth quirking up. He'd finally gotten her to stop running and to accept his meager offer of help. What came after that, he couldn't say, but that was a question for another day. Today, this was enough.

Tomorrow or perhaps the next day, he'd begin tackling the next set of questions about his future and how that intersected with hers.

———

AUBREY STARED in the looking glass in her shop and bit her lip. She looked every inch the kept woman tonight.

Four days had passed since she'd accepted Nick's offer of help and she'd questioned her decision a thousand times since then. Why had she agreed?

Because she had to purchase that diamond now. She'd gone too far down the path to turn back. For the first time since she'd started this journey, Aubrey wondered what happened if she failed tonight. If she didn't get the stone.

Would she simply return Mr. Smith's money and then ask for the deed back? Did it work like that? Nervous tension rose up in her stomach as she remembered his threats and the way he'd broken her spectacles. What had she gotten herself into, precisely?

She shook her head, focusing on her gown. It clung to her curves in the most flattering way, the blue-green silk shimmering in the candlelight. She'd loosely pinned her hair, highlighting its thickness, and the few trailing pieces only made her fragile features appear more so. She had to look the part of Nick's paramour in order to make her appearance believable. But she had chosen a more modest neckline. Her bosom was ample, and she'd not put it on display for a rake, no matter what he'd promised.

She didn't wish to invite other men to attempt to seek out her company, either. If Nick could find her, then so could another, and the last she thing she needed was more male attention. She didn't even want Nick's.

Not really. Well, perhaps just a little. In those quiet moments, the girl who loved him still liked to whisper that he was as handsome as ever and far less cocksure. If anything, he seemed...*insecure* wasn't the right word. He was as insistent as ever, his shoulders broad and straight. But he'd done a great deal more reflection in the past few days than he'd done in the two years she'd lived near him as a child.

Which wasn't fair. Children weren't all that self-aware. She hadn't been.

But she'd expected him to have the same swagger. Instead, he'd shared regrets, and even significant remorse for his past deeds.

But she'd not allow those secret little wishes to distract her. She'd decided not to marry for a very good reason. Several. What man had she ever been able to trust? And despite Nick's more vulnerable side, he'd been part of the mold that had created her.

He'd always had times he'd seemed more sympathetic than the others. He'd actually spent time talking with her, laughing with her. But then when his friends had teased her, he'd laughed along with them.

She straightened her shoulders as the shop bell sounded

TAMMY ANDRESEN

behind her.

"Damn." She heard his deep rumble, felt it move through her as he followed up the word with an appreciative whistle. "Aubrey, you look stunning. I mean…"

She turned to look at him, some of her loose curls cascading over her shoulder. "My mother knew how to look good. She made sure I did as well." At least until she'd given up on her daughter.

"I'm certain she did. Honestly, I'm surprised she didn't leverage your looks into a stellar match despite your birth. There are plenty of men who would not care about your circumstances…"

Her stomach dropped. "It was her original plan. But we both know I went through a very awkward phase. It was then that she sold the diamond for her own future, thinking that she would not be able to make a match with me that would provide for her."

His brow pinched above his nose as he stared at her.

She looked back at the glass that stood in her shop, normally for clients, but she could still see his face in the mirror. "Instead, she found me an apprenticeship with a dressmaker."

He stopped moving toward her, his gaze holding hers, as the words hung between them. "Awkward phase?"

"Don't pretend like you don't know," she said, her anger coming to her rescue. "You teased me nearly as much as your friends."

He looked her up and down, his gaze taking in every inch of her body. She did all she could not to shrink back. But then finally his gaze found her eyes again. "If you went through a phase, it's over now."

It was she who broke their stare, her face turning to the side. "It might be over, but it reverberates through my entire adult life. I am here because of those years."

"You could still marry. Men would clamor for your hand if you made yourself available—"

"I will never marry," she said to cut him off. "I will never give myself to a man, never put myself in the position to be dependent on anyone." She forced herself to stop, though part of her wished to rail against the system that had made her feel less. Always less.

36

"Never is a long time."

She looked at him again, his own features laced with pain. He shifted, running a hand through the thick waves of his dark hair. "But I have made a similar vow, so I understand."

That made her pause. "A duke who has vowed not to marry."

His brows rose. "How long did you live near my family estate?"

"Two years."

"And in that entire time, did you ever see my father or my mother?"

She gasped in a small breath. That answer was *no* and if she'd been honest, she hadn't noticed, either. She'd been so angry at him for not seeing her pain but she'd missed his. Shame made heat rise in her cheeks. "I did not."

"That village was the place my father stuffed the people of whom he'd grown tired. Me included."

"My mother too?" Her chin dropped a little. Her mother mostly hid the affairs, but she'd had them. It kept her in the latest fashion, kept servants and fine food on the table.

"I don't know for certain," he said and she pivoted so that she faced him again. His hands came to her shoulders, and slowly he turned her back to the mirror so that they could both see themselves. He held her eyes with his as he murmured close to her ear. "But whatever she did, I admire the fact that you stand tall on your own, Aubrey. You're magnificent in every way."

Why did those words make her pulse skip a beat? Fill her with gratitude? Make her so happy, as though she'd waited her entire life for that praise? "Don't do that." Even she could hear the pain in her own voice. "Please."

He slid his hands down her shoulders to lightly grasp her upper arms. "The next time you need help, you come to me. My door is always open to you."

Her breath caught. She'd been alone for so long. How had he known that's what she needed to hear? Another piece of her resolve crumbled as his bright green eyes held hers.

CHAPTER FIVE

NICK HELD her gaze in the mirror. He could see the hurt girl under the strong woman and it tore him to pieces.

He knew there was a hurt boy inside him too. But in so many ways, he'd been blessed where she hadn't. He wanted to hold her close, comfort her.

But he could give her something she'd been striving for...the Rivermore Diamond. He'd done some research at his preferred jeweler. He'd wondered at first if the stone was actually paste, but it was not. And then, as he'd listened, he learned that the stone was a rare blue diamond, set over one hundred years earlier, and prized for its unique blue color and clarity. At nearly five carats, it was a prize, to be certain. And it was likely to sell for a small fortune. Her shop did well but he had to wonder—how might a dressmaker afford such a treasure?

"Shall we go? We've got places to be and diamonds to buy."

That won him a small smile as one of her hands came atop the one he'd placed on her arm. "Thank you, Nick."

The soft way she said his name made his muscles tighten and he squeezed her arms. He wanted to step close, bury his face in her hair, promise her the world.

He let go of her, sliding his fingers from hers as he took a step back. "Do you know the history of the stone?'

She shook her head. "No. I don't know much about it other than what I remember from my childhood."

"What sort of memories?"

He saw the slight wilt in her shoulders and he reached for her hand, placing her fingers in his elbow. Slowly, they began moving toward the door.

"My mother telling me it was a gift from my father to secure my future. Her wearing it when she was between benefactors. The day she sold it for half of what it was worth."

"You know its worth?"

"Four thousand pounds, give or take," she answered with a grimace. "And hopefully not too much more because six thousand is all I have. I'd hoped..."

He was impressed she had that amount. "Auctions can be tricky. It depends on how much the seller knows about the piece and how fanciful the buyers are. Is one of them willing to overpay?"

She gave a tight nod. "Those are the next problems. The first one was getting to the auction."

He opened the door, leading her to his carriage. After helping her inside, he climbed in too. He didn't bother to tell her he'd cover the difference. She'd only refuse. That much he knew. But he'd not leave tonight without the stone, and after he'd acquired the diamond, he'd decide how best to continue their relationship.

Because he didn't want to let her go. Not yet. He was learning so much about her and about himself too. The restlessness had calmed the day after he'd left her shop but had grown with each day they'd been apart.

But here in her company now, he'd quieted again. And the past year of spending his time in reflective solitude didn't seem like a vague notion of a life lived wrong but a definite step toward a better future.

He'd given up his old life to prepare for the new.

What exactly that *new* was, he wasn't sure, but he knew this...

Aubrey was a part of that life. He could say that for certain. Now, to convince her…

The carriage began to rumble down the street, a quiet settling between them. He stared at her as she sat in the forward-facing seat, her hands tightly clasped, looking out the window.

He didn't interrupt her thoughts; instead, he took the opportunity to drink in every detail of her face, the changes the years had brought, the beauty she'd become. The brash girl who'd turned into a strong, enchanting woman. He drank in her high cheekbones, full lips, the graceful line of her neck, the swell of her breasts. He ached to touch her again but he held his hands still in his lap as the silence stretched on.

They arrived at the home of Lord Hampstead, making their way up the stairs with a number of other guests.

Several sets of male eyes drifted to Aubrey, each man assessing her as though she were another jewel up for auction.

Inadvertently, he pulled her closer. For the first time he considered if he'd done her some harm in bringing her here. Would men assume she was available to be their mistress? At least her identity seemed reasonably hidden in that dress shop. After tonight, she'd regain her anonymity. A tight coif and a pair of spectacles and no one noticed the beauty in plain sight.

Fools.

But tonight, he'd stay close to her side. He had no intention of allowing any of these men to hurt her.

He realized she'd cared for herself for a long time, but he couldn't help but feel protective of her now.

They made their way into the entry, notably clear of the usual artwork that adorned a lord's home, and started up the grand stairs.

Nick had done some research on Lord Hampstead as well. A heavy gambler and lavish spender, he seemed to be in a great deal of debt and was currently out of favor with the queen. Nick could only hope that meant the man was desperate enough to let the diamond go at a reasonable price.

They entered the music room, where rows of chairs had been

arranged to face a podium. Men and a few women assembled in the room, everyone's voices hushed as they chose a seat.

The collection was extensive and of great value. Nick recognized several of the lords and ladies in attendance.

In the back sat a fair number of men in more practical attire, his own solicitor among them. They each likely represented a lord or lady and they'd do the bidding for their patron.

Aubrey shifted next to him as a man stepped up to the podium. "Thank you all for coming."

Nick gave her fingers the slightest squeeze of comfort as a maid walked in carrying the first piece on a pillow.

Then the auctioneer cleared his throat. "Shall we begin?"

———

AUBREY'S NERVES jangled with each new piece that was brought out for bidding. She couldn't say whether the jewels were going for reasonable prices or not. This entire affair had been foisted upon her with little time to prepare.

She felt a bit like she was drowning. How would she succeed and what would happen if she did not?

Next to her, Nick shifted. "That was an excellent value," he murmured.

She blinked and then drew in a deep breath. "You know that ring's value?"

He nodded. "It's worth far more than it just sold for. Makes me hopeful."

"How do you know that?" she asked, turning to him and forgetting her nerves.

He gave her that smile that she both hated and loved. "I spoke with my jeweler yesterday. He knew all about the auction. In fact, he's here, I believe, bidding as well."

She took a small breath of surprise. That fact that he'd done research calmed her, but the sheer number of people here who were more knowledgeable and bidding frightened her. "I'm not going to win the necklace, am I?" Her palms began to sweat. Why hadn't she considered all this sooner?

"Don't give up now," he whispered close to her ear. "You've come this far."

She gave a tight nod as she straightened her shoulders. He was right. But as she looked to her right, she drank in his profile. "Thank you for coming with me."

"You're welcome," he said as he looked at her again, his green eyes sparkling in the candlelight.

"I'm glad you're here," she whispered, genuinely meaning the words. He'd been a help in so many ways.

"Me too."

But conversation stopped as the next pillow appeared in a new maid's arms, the Rivermore Diamond resting on its velvet folds. The blue diamond was surrounded by white diamonds and strung on a necklace of pearls. Even in the dim light, it twinkled and winked as the candlelight bounced off its cut façade.

She gasped, recognizing the details intimately, memories of the necklace on her mother filling her thoughts and choking off her air.

"Will you bid for me? Please?" Aubrey asked as she leaned into the strength of his arm, barely able to push out the words. She could hardly catch her breath as the full weight of what she'd done truly bore down on her. She had no idea what would happen if she failed...

"Of course," he said as the piece was set in front of the auctioneer, the man describing the weight and setting, craftmanship, and clarity of the stone.

"Shall we begin at one thousand pounds?"

From the back, a hand quickly rose.

Aubrey winced. Clearly there was other interest.

Nick raised his hand several times as the price quickly climbed from the single thousands to the two thousands to the threes.

Slowly, bidders fell off, but one man in the back—she didn't know if he was a jeweler or solicitor—kept upping Nick's bid until they were approaching four thousand and the amount she did not wish to surpass. The extra funds from Mr. Smith would allow her to grow her business and create a solid profit for herself. She could go higher, of course. She'd still gain her shop, but…

Her breath held in her throat as Nick called out, "Three thousand nine hundred."

She reached for his forearm, holding it in her grasp as she waited to see if the other man would bid.

"Four thousand," the other man called and all the air left her lungs.

She tapped him. "Higher." She'd have to spend the reserve. If she didn't acquire the stone, Mr. Smith would expose her.

On it went until the stone passed five thousand, and then in a moment that sent her stomach crashing to the floor, it passed six thousand pounds. The room grew suffocatingly hot as she clutched at Nick's arm.

Her heart hammered in her chest, her eyes blurred. She'd lost the stone.

Even worse, she'd have to face Mr. Smith. Was she in danger? She had his money still, she could return it…

But he'd warned her not to fail. What would happen when she told him that she had? She looked over at Nick. He'd promised her help? Would he aid her in this? Could he help her buy the stone? Protect her from Mr. Smith? Did she even dare ask?

Did she admit to him the deal she'd made to try and salvage her future? Shame filled her. And then there was the fact that it was dangerous to rely on Nick.

He'd already removed several of her defenses and if she weren't careful…

He'd have her breaking all her rules. The one carefully in place to never make her feel like ugly Ducky again.

But if she didn't rely on Nick, what would happen with Mr. Smith?

She drew in a trembling gulp of air, half aware that the bidding had continued.

"Eight thousand pounds," the auctioneer called out. "Do I have eight thousand five hundred?"

Silence fell across the room as Aubrey held in a low moan. Could the people around them hear her heart breaking?

Her throat closed and she leaned into Nick, her forehead coming to rest on the hard edge of his shoulder.

"Eight thousand it is," the auctioneer's voice echoed over the room. "Bring out the next piece."

Clapping filled the high ceilings of the music room as Aubrey sank further into her chair.

"Do you wish to stay for the rest of the auction?"

"No," she said, her voice catching even on that single word.

"All right, then. Let's go collect your necklace."

Her head snapped up as she met his gaze, hers surely colored with confusion. Her necklace? Collect? What did he mean?

CHAPTER SIX

NICK SAW her confusion and he couldn't help but smile. She'd had no idea, of course, that his solicitor had taken up bidding against the other competitor.

He looked back at the man who'd bid first against him and then against his solicitor, but his brow furrowed as he realized the man who'd been his competitor was already gone.

That was odd. Had the other man only been interested in the necklace? That must be the case; why else would he have left?

But a bit of unease tightened his stomach as he stood and helped Aubrey up out of her seat. Once again, several sets of eyes were cast her way.

He met the stare of the Earl of Evington, whose gaze filled with open interest and unbridled want.

Nick's hand tightened on Aubrey's.

They quickly stepped into the hall, his solicitor following them out.

"Nick?" she asked, her hand gripping his forearm.

"This is Mister Hanson, my solicitor." Nick did not tell the other man Aubrey's name. Mr. Hanson was the definition of discreet, but he might risk someone else overhearing. He'd not do anything that would bring any more danger to Aubrey. It was imperative that he protect her from this world. She had no one else to keep her safe here.

"Pleased to make your acquaintance." Hanson gave a short bow and then began leading the way down the hall away from the music room to a smaller sitting room.

Aubrey and Nick entered, remaining near the door as Mr. Hanson crossed the space and began to speak to another man who was bent over several pillows adorned with various jewels. Even Nick paused to see the collection displayed in such a way. His solicitor stepped back and the other man gave a nod, waving a maid forward. Carefully, she grabbed the pillow with the Rivermore Diamond necklace.

Aubrey's hand tapped at his arm. "What have you done?" she whispered. The others were several feet away and he turned into her to keep their discussion private.

"I got you your necklace," he said, just a bit of pride making his chest puff out. A man felt good about giving a woman what she most wanted.

But when her gaze met his, she hardly looked grateful. In fact, a bit of fear shone in her eyes, punctuated by her next words. "I can't accept a gift like that."

He leaned back, shock making his lips part. "Are you upset with me? For giving you what you most wanted?"

From the depths of her dress a fan emerged. Did she have a pocket? But he hardly had time to inspect the dress when the wooden handle came down on his wrist. "Now everyone in that room is certain I'm your paramour."

"They were already certain," he answered, turning half toward her. "They could be certain while you had no necklace or certain with the jewel in your possession, but I thought you'd prefer the latter."

"You shouldn't have," she added, her skin distressingly pale. "I don't know that I can accept such a gift from anyone."

Well, that was just...ungrateful? Accurate? "Did you want the necklace or not?"

She shook her head. "I wanted it, yes. But..." Her words trailed off. "I just don't know what this means."

His jaw hardened. She was right, of course. A single woman accepting a gift from a man was a public declaration that she belonged to him. And while he'd prefer all those men in that room thinking that Aubrey was under his protection, he could see how that fact might be distressing to her. She'd been careful to never link herself to a man.

He scowled. "I didn't mean…" He let out a rumbling breath. "I'm sorry."

He felt her soften. "Thank you for saying that."

"The problem is that I am now the owner of the necklace."

She smiled then, further relaxing. "It's a problem I'll take over the alternative."

"So you'll allow me to gift you the necklace?"

"Oh no," she answered. "Of course not."

Of course not. He wasn't certain if he should rumble in dissatisfaction or laugh. He could say one thing about Aubrey—she was ever interesting.

"Then what do you propose?"

She paused as she bit her lip, staring up at him with those large, expressive blue eyes. "I'm not certain yet. I need a moment to think."

Mr. Hanson approached them, a box in hand. Carefully, he handed the box to Nick. "Your Grace."

Nick took the box, gently removing the lid. The Rivermore Diamond winked up at him, nestled in its bed of silk.

He felt the jolt that traveled through Aubrey and then she reached out a hand. "May I?"

"Please do."

And then she reached out her gloved fingers, sliding them along the top of the stone. "It's as stunning as I remember."

"It pales in comparison to you," he replied before he'd thought the words through.

Mr. Hanson cleared his throat, determinedly looking to his left to study the wallpaper or perhaps a nearby lamp.

"Thank you." Aubrey gave him another soft smile, the sort that was slowly working its way into every corner of his heart.

"You're welcome," he returned.

47

"If that is all, Your Grace?" Mr. Hanson asked.

He started to say yes but Aubrey's hand tightened on his arm once again. He looked down at her as she bit her lips.

"Perhaps we could come to an agreement for the sale of the stone from you to me? Mister Hanson could write up the details?" she asked.

He stared at her. She ought to take the necklace as a gift, keep her money, and be well set for her future. But he could see that she'd not allow him to just gift her the stone. With a quick nod, he put the lid on the box again. "I'm sure we can come to an agreement. But if you don't mind, I'd like to allow Mister Hanson to return home, it's quite late. Tomorrow, we'll meet at his office after we've had a chance to negotiate."

She nodded her agreement as Mr. Hanson left the room. And then he handed the box to Aubrey. Because he wanted her to spend time remembering how much she wanted that stone before she heard his terms...

————

THE ENTIRE CARRIAGE RIDE HOME, Aubrey stared at the diamond. She'd removed the lid as soon as the carriage had begun to move. The interior of the carriage was dark, only lit by the swinging lamps that hung about the vehicle, but it still winked up at her, flashing in its brilliance.

"I'd forgotten how large it is," she murmured. Then her gaze was cast to his. "I can't believe I didn't do more research. Thank you for thinking to do so."

He leaned forward. "I am used to making large purchases, where you are not."

That was the truth. And the reminder that she was far out of her element.

Had she been a fool not to accept the necklace as a present? She could keep the money, give Mr. Smith the necklace, and get the deed to her shop.

But she was a woman who didn't take the charity of men and the strings that might be attached to it.

Well, she had been that woman. Now, with Mr. Smith about to make another trip to her shop, she wondered how best to protect herself.

She cast her gaze to Nick. She had no doubt that he could keep her safe. Did she need that protection? Would Mr. Smith honor their bargain even if she delivered the necklace? It seemed she solved one problem only to realize there was another. But she knew enough about men to understand that when one forced a woman to do his bidding, he wasn't to be trusted.

She nipped at her lip. "What are your terms for transferring the necklace to me?"

Nick stared back at her, his gaze so penetrating, she was certain he saw all the details she was trying to hide. "Why don't you begin? You won't allow me to gift you the necklace."

"No," she whispered, looking down at it again. What would she tell Mr. Smith when he asked for it?

It wasn't that she didn't wish to take it. She did. But she was afraid of the future consequences. Every interaction with men she'd ever had had taught her to be leery. There were always consequences when one accepted help or gifts. Wasn't her mother's life proof enough? She'd been used by so many men in exchange for a few baubles or coins. Aubrey would never be that woman.

"So you wish to purchase the stone from me?"

That was the only option. "Yes. That's correct."

"And how long do you think it would take you to acquire the additional funds?"

She shook her head. Years. That was the answer. Her shoulders drooped. "And you'd give me the stone after I've collected the funds?"

"Something like that," he answered, leaning forward so that his elbows rested on his knees. "Or, I could make you a different sort of offer."

Her breath caught.

He was going to ask her to be his mistress. Bile rose in her throat.

She hated the idea of being used by a man. Even she could acknowledge that of all the men she'd ever met, Nick was the one she was most enamored with and that he'd been nothing but honorable this past week, but still...

She'd danced this dance before. She'd be used and forgotten. Hadn't she seen her mother do this set of steps time and time again?

"I don't want your offer."

"Are you certain?" he asked, pushing further out on the seat. "Don't you think you should hear it first?"

"A man's offer landed me in this predicament to begin with. The last thing I need—"

"A man's offer?"

Drat. What had she gone and done? She'd been talking about Mr. Smith, but did she tell Nick about him? Embroil the duke in her problems even further? How indebted to Nick would she be if she did? "My father, my mother, the necklace..."

He grimaced, sliding a hand through his hair. "Right."

She looked down at the necklace. Then again, whatever price Nick charged, it had to be better than facing Mr. Smith alone. "But..."

"But what?" He scooted forward again. "Aubrey..." And then he reached out and grasped her hand in his. She shivered to feel his touch and her eyes fluttered closed.

If she were being honest, there was another reason she resisted. It would be so easy to fall into this man and forget everything that was important to her. Allow him to break her heart yet again.

He would. At some point he'd grow bored, move on to a new conquest. She'd never be enough for him.

She'd never even been enough for her own father. "It's nothing," she whispered. "I can sell my shop to pay you, at least in part. It would make you my landlord but..."

His hand tightened. "You'd allow me to be your landlord? You, who likes to rely on no men?"

That did seem out of character. But she had to find a way to get Mr. Smith the necklace without completely compromising her entire future.

"I could…" She hesitated. She needed Nick's protection. That was clear. She'd not thought beyond getting the necklace, but now… She swallowed down a lump.

She had to compromise somewhere to ensure her own safety, her future. But did she risk becoming what she disliked most in order to do that? If she acquired the necklace for Mr. Smith, she'd at least have all the means necessary to care for herself and any consequences of a union with Nick. "Aubrey, what are you working yourself up to ask?"

He slid from his seat, crossing the small distance to sit next to her. His arm came about her shoulders and suddenly she was engulfed in his size, his muscles, his scent…sandalwood and leather. She breathed deeply, closing her eyes. "I need…"

"Tell me," he asked, pulling her closer. Her body tingled in all the places it touched his. Which made her request easier.

"I want…" she murmured so low, she didn't even know if he heard her. He reached up a hand, tracing her cheek with the pad of his thumb. Her eyes fluttered closed once again. Her actions were justified. The point of remaining independent was to keep herself from harm. She was not going do that by pushing Nick away now.

He was so close when he whispered, "I'll do whatever I can."

"I want to be your—" But her words halted when a loud blast filled the night, deafening her and cutting off her voice.

CHAPTER SEVEN

NICK'S HEAD snapped up when the carriage gave a wild veer to the left.

His footmen began yelling to one another and he caught enough of the words to know that the shot had been aimed at their carriage.

The reins snapped and the carriage jolted forward, as he wrapped his arms about Aubrey, pulling her tightly to his chest. She burrowed against him, her arms circling his waist as she pressed deeper into his side.

Another shot rang out, closer, and his head cocked to the side as one of the footmen yelled, "Got him."

But then another blast rent the air. Nick lifted Aubrey, settling her on the floor between the benches. He lifted the seat of the rear-facing bench and pulled out a pistol of his own. Quickly loading the gun, he looked down at Aubrey. "Don't move."

"Nick," she cried, her eyes round as saucers as she looked up at him. He gave her what he hoped was a reassuring smile, stepping over her and opening the carriage door. Popping his head out, he could see that three men followed them on horseback.

Levelling his pistol, he took aim and fired.

He saw the bullet hit, the man on the left jerking back as his horse instantly slowed.

Nick ducked back into the carriage to reload.

"Who's behind us?" Aubrey gasped as she partially sat up.

"Two men on horseback. Stay down," he answered, stuffing the pistol full of powder.

"Who are they?"

"Damned if I know, but you'd better bet I'll find out."

He made to step over her again, fire another shot, when she called out to him again. "Nick."

There was something urgent and honest in the way she said his name. It was a plea but also an admission. Did she know who those men were?

His stomach dropped and he halted for a moment. He looked down at her, the guilt in her face affirming his suspicion.

His jaw clenched. He'd been a bloody fool. As he'd held her hand, he'd had visions of a future with her. Granted, he'd thought himself never to wed, but his thoughts were more of a vague idea and less of an actual plan. Besides, marrying someone like Audrey was its own punishment to his father, while Nick himself didn't give a wit about her birth.

Marriage was the perfect solution in some ways. Or so it had seemed. He'd finally met a woman who'd made his life worthwhile.

He should have known that she'd been playing him all along. His gut wrenched again even as he pushed open the door and fired another shot.

This one swung wide and didn't hit either rider, so he snapped the door shut again.

"Open the gate," his driver shouted in the night.

Distantly, he heard the gates squeaking open and then moments later, the carriage barreled past iron doors, and then they slammed shut behind the carriage.

He slumped down on the seat, setting the pistol aside and then dragging his hands down his face as he tried to process all that had just happened.

He'd been about to break his lifelong rule for a woman who'd been using him all along. How very typical.

"Nick?" she whispered, touching his knee. "Are you all right?"

"Fine," he answered automatically. Only his pride and perhaps his feelings had been wounded, after all.

"I…" she started. "Where are we?"

"My home."

"Oh," she said, using his leg to lift herself from the floor. Automatically, he reached out to help her. "I see."

He ought to send her on her way. Let her face whatever mess she'd made on her own, but as he opened his eyes, they met hers, worry pulling her face into taut lines, her hand shaking in his.

"You're going to tell me everything."

She nodded.

"Sit."

She did as he commanded, which in and of itself was odd. The carriage rolled to a stop, the door snapping open. "Your Grace," one of his footmen called. "Are you hurt?"

"I'm fine, Simmons. Is it safe to go inside?"

"Yes, Your Grace."

With a tight nod, he exited the carriage, reaching his hand for Aubrey's. She took it, holding the box with the Rivermore Diamond in her other arm.

"They wanted that, didn't they?" he asked, the first piece of the puzzle falling into place.

"I didn't see the men who chased us so I couldn't say for certain, but my guess is yes."

"And who would you wager might have been chasing us? Because my guess is that you have far more knowledge on this topic than myself."

He held her hand walking up the stairs, where the doors swept open. "I don't know who he is for certain but…"

"Aubrey, my patience is wearing terribly thin. Start talking. I mean it."

He pulled her toward the sitting room just off the entry, the one he knew was stocked with whiskey.

Letting her go, he crossed the room to the decanter and pulled out a glass, pouring himself a healthy tumbler.

He hadn't had the burning liquid in months, but tonight…

"I'll take one of those too, please," Aubrey said behind him. "If you don't mind."

He did as she asked, pouring her a far smaller glass. Turning, he handed her the drink, noting that her fingers still trembled. Then he gestured for her to sit, taking the chair across from her.

Only the fire lit the room, burning low in the grate. She did as commanded, smoothing her skirts and then taking a tiny sip from the glass he'd given her.

He heard her faint choke, but she kept the liquid down.

"All right, Aubrey. Enough stalling. Begin."

———

BEGIN. Guilt ate at her stomach. Nick's carriage had been shot at because of her.

But to start talking was easier said than done. For a moment she considered what she might share, but it didn't take long. "A little over a week ago, a man arrived at my shop just as I was closing, much like you did the other day."

"I see."

"He…" She took another drink, needing something to do as she spoke. "He'd collected the deed to my shop and he claimed that if I wanted to stay in business…" Her voice trailed off. "He knew my real name, knew who my father was, knew that I'd once been in possession of the diamond years ago. He claimed that I needed to get the stone for him and then he gave me the money—"

"That's how you got the four thousand pounds?"

"Six," she whispered. "'Mister Smith' was the name on the deed below the old owner's, and he said if I got the stone, I could have whatever money was left over and I'd own my own shop."

"And you just dragged me into this?"

She sat up straighter, indignation replacing some of her guilt. "I did not drag you. In fact, I'm fairly certain you inserted yourself. I tried to refuse your help—several times."

He blinked in surprise, setting his half-empty glass aside. "That's true, I suppose."

"You suppose?" she asked, shaking her head. "Which part is less than clear?"

"The part where you made it seem like you wanted the stone for yourself."

"Oh." She slumped back down. "That part."

His jaw hardened and it was her turn to scrub her face. "I'm an excellent seamstress. One of the best. But by the time I pay my rent and expenses, I never seem to get ahead. This was my chance, or so I thought, to actually be in possession of my life."

"I see."

"I don't want to marry, which you well know." She took another large swallow and then set the drink aside.

"Neither did I."

She caught the use of the past tense and she started in surprise. "You do now?"

"Not really," he answered. "Please continue."

"His offer would mean that I would have the shop and a nest egg."

"How did you not know that he'd never honor the bargain?" Nick asked, his fist clenching.

She cleared her throat. "I'm new at intrigue."

"And why did you not tell me sooner so I could have better protected us both?"

"Because," she said, her voice trembling just loud enough for both of them to hear, "I didn't know I could trust you. I'm just the ugly girl who no one wanted."

There was a heavy pause, the air weighted with her words, his silence, before he finally spoke again. "I want you."

The air rushed from her lungs. She knew that already. But to hear it so plainly, it brought a tear slipping down her cheek. "That is different. No one wants me. The whole me. Not really."

His jaw worked and then he was up on his feet, standing in front of her. "I know the feeling. No one wants me, either."

Her mouth fell open. It wasn't true. Ever since she'd met him, everyone wanted him. But she didn't have time to say that he was wrong, because he was pulling her up out of the chair and against his chest.

The hard muscles rippled against her softer flesh, causing her to shiver with delight.

"I've wanted you since the first moment I laid eyes on you in that ballroom, and I want you more with each passing moment we spend together."

She filled her lungs with his scent as she tried to remind herself to stay strong. He wanted her for now. Physical desire was completely different from the emotional bond she spoke of.

But this is what she'd been about to ask him for. An affair for a necklace. Well, perhaps that had shifted. Now it was an affair for protection.

But still.

She'd compromise on this one principle to keep herself safe and preserve her independent future.

His mouth dropped closer as he brought a hand up to her cheek. "Do you still want me to leave you be?"

"No," she answered honestly. "I'm sorry I endangered you today. I never meant—"

"I've already moved on," he said with that smile. The one that always stole her breath. "What I need to decide now is how best to keep you safe."

She slid her hands up his arm, feeling the muscles tense beneath his coat. She hadn't even offered herself yet. Was the bargain assumed? Did she ask?

She didn't want to think, just to feel. Today had been one event after another, her emotions sliding up and down with each twist and turn. She didn't wish to reason any more today.

Being with Nick had saved her life tonight. The weight of that settled over her as his forehead came to hers. What was more, the

Rivermore Diamond sat on the chair she'd just exited. "Nick." His name tumbled from her lips, half a plea, as she looked into the depths of his eyes. No wonder women allowed this man to ruin them.

Being held like this, looked at like this, protected. It was intoxicating. Or was that the whiskey?

His thumb stroked down her cheek and over her bottom lip. "You can't go home tonight."

They were going to have an affair. Part of her jolted in surprised delight while another part cried that she had given up on her resolve. She pushed that voice back down.

"I'll have a guest room readied for you."

A guest room?

And then slowly, he eased back. "I think we should both get some sleep and then we can further discuss how to proceed."

Proceed? "With what?"

He still held her waist and he stopped pulling away as he met her gaze. "We need to know who this Smith is and why he tried to hurt you when you were about to deliver the diamond."

Both excellent questions and the last ones on her mind. What she was far more concerned about was where she stood with a certain duke.

CHAPTER EIGHT

NICK'S BODY raged with objection. He'd held a compliant Aubrey in his arms. Why hadn't he kissed her, done more than that?

Now she was tucked in her guest room and he was trapped in his own chamber and as far from sleep as a man could be.

Should her pour himself another whiskey?

He shook his head. He'd feel worse in the morning for it than if he stayed up the whole of the night sober.

Perhaps some exercise would do him good. He'd gone from the auction, to a chase with shots fired, to holding the woman he was falling in love with in his arms.

And he was falling in love. Though it had never happened to him before, he knew that's what this was. The very fact that he'd been so hurt at the sniff of betrayal was all the proof he needed.

But in addition to understanding what was happening to him, he also knew with startling clarity that he was not ready to admit any of this to Aubrey. His reaction to the idea that she'd tricked him had been immediate and gut-wrenching.

He'd been too scarred by his parents to give himself away just yet. He had to place his relationship with Aubrey on more stable ground before he exposed himself with that kind of vulnerability.

But that required time. And in order to gain time, he needed to deal with this Mr. Smith and keep Aubrey safe.

He opened his bedroom door and started back down the stairs to the sitting room he'd left not an hour ago. The glass of whiskey he'd left on the table had already been cleared, but he crossed to the buffet, serving another one. He might feel terrible tomorrow, but at least he'd get a bit of respite from his swirling thoughts.

"Couldn't sleep either?"

He twisted around. Aubrey was curled in the same chair, her feet tucked under her, her hand wrapped about a glass. "What are you doing here?"

She shrugged. "It's the only room in the house I know, and my mind is so full..."

He poured his glass and settled across from her. Her hair was now in a loose braid that accentuated the thick blonde waves. The tones of her skin were warm and the housecoat she wore was belted tightly around her waist. What was underneath?

Every muscle clenched as he shifted. This type of thinking would not help. "Mine too."

She unfolded herself from the chair, crossing to the fire and leaning her arm against the high mantle, her forehead coming to rest on her arm. "How are we going to find Smith?"

He stood too, more than happy to be closer to her. The dressing gown followed the curves of her body, and he longed to trace them with his hand.

"We'll start with that deed. If he bought the shop, a solicitor oversaw the sale. My solicitor will find him."

She straightened, turning toward him. "Of course."

He scratched his chin as he stared into the fire, coming to stand next to her. "What I don't understand is why Smith sent you to purchase the stone. It's such an overly complicated plan. Why not just send in a solicitor?"

She gasped as she looked at him. "I don't know. I didn't even think..." She shook her head. "Nick. Thank you." And then she touched his arm, her fingers sliding along his biceps.

He didn't think, he just reached out, hooking her waist with his hand and pulling her close to his body.

Without her stays and his jacket, her body settled into his, molding to his frame.

He slid a hand along her jaw, cupping her cheek in his palm. It was too much, her beauty in the moonlight, the appreciation, the fact that she needed him. He wanted to be everything for her.

Her protector, lover, husband. He understood her desire to be alone. Her parents had been atrocious.

But they understood each other's hurt. He lowered his mouth until his lips hovered just above hers. "Aubrey."

"Nick." Her fingers danced over his shirt, settling around his neck before sliding up into the hair just above his collar. "I know I'm not..."

He didn't wish to hear whatever she might say. Something about not being good enough. But to his mind, there was no one better.

He brushed his mouth across hers, their lips barely touching, but somehow that only created more sensation.

She gasped underneath him and he nearly smiled to know she was just as affected. So he repeated the touch.

Another gentle brush and then another, until she was rising on her tiptoes to chase his lips.

So odd—as children she'd chased him. He'd always liked her but she'd been too young then. And this time, he'd been chasing her.

But now, as she rose, he came down, and they met precisely in the middle. He increased the pressure of the kiss, giving her the exact kiss he knew she wanted.

He heard her low moan, her lips so pliant under his that desire made his manhood heavy.

He lifted his head, just to look in the clear blue of her eyes, see the passion that surely filled him. It was there, but with it...

"You look confused."

Her tongue darted out as she licked her lips. The lust that was building in him swelled again.

"I am, a bit."

"Why?"

She shook her head, her fingertips digging into his scalp. "Because…"

And then she looked away.

————

How did a woman tell a man she'd never been kissed before?

At one and twenty, she wondered if her lack of experience was odd. She'd been too busy and too determined to avoid any behavior that might lead her to repeat her mother's mistakes.

"Tell me why you're confused. Did you not expect to like kissing me?"

Her cheeks flamed with heat. "I didn't expect anything. I've never…" Her words trailed off, but she watched realization dawn in his eyes.

"Never?" he asked, sliding his other hand up her back and over her neck so that he held her face in both hands.

She gave a little shake to her chin, as much as she could between his hands. "I didn't want to do anything that might compromise my goals."

He leaned down again, giving her another achingly soft brush of his lips. Those tender kisses made her ache with want. Was it always like this?

"I understand," he whispered. "And I'm honored to be the exception."

She started to speak but then closed her mouth again. He'd always been the exception. He was the first and only man she'd ever wanted and that had not diminished as she indulged in their kiss.

How could she resist the man who stood between her and the force that wished to harm her? And besides, she couldn't deny that there was a part of her that wanted him.

She could justify all she wished, but it was the truth.

"We're meeting with my solicitor tomorrow. Originally, the contract we were going to create was for the necklace, but that is far less important now."

Aubrey was glad she got to see the necklace again. The piece was a part of her past, her history. Nick had taken the necklace and placed it in his safe, which is where it would likely stay. She had no idea what would happen to the money she still had in her possession, but he was right.

She'd been a fool to hope.

A thought slashed through her mind, causing pain to radiate out from her chest. Would Nick give the necklace to his wife someday?

He had insinuated his position on marriage was changing. The idea of another woman wearing the necklace because Nick gave it to her made her ache.

She drew in a deep breath, looking toward the fire. "So we'll have him start the investigation on Mister Smith instead?"

"That's right."

"It makes sense." She didn't ask about the necklace. It wasn't hers to enquire after. "After the meeting, I'll have to go to my shop."

"Your shop?" He gave her a fierce scowl.

"I have to live," she said, leaning back to look him in the face. "Without work, I can't survive."

"Precisely. You have to live. You're not going to the shop. He's been there before."

She understood his point. She did. "But without an occupation, I'll starve."

He slid his hands down her back, settling them around her waist, seeming to span the entirety of it. "I would never allow you to starve."

"You're already helping me with the investigation. You can't support me as well. It's just not..."

She saw the understanding flare in his eyes. "Can you trust me for now? Know that I would never leave you without a way to feed yourself?"

She did trust him, but Aubrey just wasn't certain she wanted to. With each step, she seemed to lose a bit more of all she'd worked so hard to gain. "I do."

"Good," he answered as his hands slid lower, tracing her hips.

Something about his hands so close to the aching junction between her legs made her gasp.

Her body had very different goals from her mind.

"I'm glad you trust me," he said, his mouth sliding close to her ear as he spoke. "I know it's difficult for both of us."

He'd mentioned his parents before. "Tell me about your childhood."

His cheek pressed to hers. "I already told you, they were as uninterested in me as they were in each other. I rarely saw them, not even for holidays, and when I did, they mostly just fought with one another."

Her heart ached a bit as their chests pressed together. "Nick, that's awful. As much as my father made me feel unwanted and my mother made me feel unattractive, she was there, at least."

He moved his head, the stubble on his cheek rubbing against her smoother skin. "You don't have to comfort me. I know your situation was worse."

"Let's not do that—quantify our losses and declare one of us a winner of the worst childhood."

She felt his smile until he pulled back to look in her eyes again. "Good idea."

"What we do know is that we actually understand each other."

"Well said." He caressed her hips, his hands moving slowly back up to her waist. "And what I can promise you is that I'll protect you."

She closed her eyes as his lips came down over hers again. The feel of his mouth emptied her mind of any arguments she might have made.

She knew he was right. Going to the shop left her vulnerable. But her business was the very thing she'd been attempting to protect, grow.

She broke away from the kiss, looking up into his eyes. "Could I work on some of my gowns here? I know I can't see new customers, but surely I could see the orders I've already taken filled."

He gave a slow nod, though something in his gaze was unreadable. Did he not like the idea?

"I'll send my footman over to collect whatever you need. We'll hire a courier to deliver the gowns." And then he stepped away. "But we're not going to accomplish any of these goals without some sleep. This time, I think we ought to go upstairs and actually go to bed."

She gave him a small smile and then a quick nod, butterflies dancing in her stomach. Would he join her?

"Do you remember the way to your room?"

She did. And she was mostly relieved she'd be going to a room of her own. But some small piece of her wondered…

Then she shook her head. Nick was helping her and that was what was important. And they had a plan for tomorrow. What happened after that, she couldn't say. One day at a time. That was the best she could hope for right now.

CHAPTER NINE

NICK WOKE WITH THE SUN, having gotten precious little sleep. Not that it mattered. He came instantly awake, infused with energy.

His first thought was of the kiss. Her mouth pressed to his had gone a long way in erasing the doubts that had plagued him earlier in the evening.

He'd nearly proposed again. She was worried about being able to provide food for herself? As his duchess, she'd never worry like that again.

But then he grimaced. She didn't wish to wed. And while most women would gladly wed him, she was not one of them. And then there were his own doubts, still plucking at the back of his thoughts.

So, he'd held his tongue. For now.

After rising, he bathed and dressed, not bothering with his valet. He needed quiet to think as he considered all he'd learned so far about the plot around Aubrey. Mentally, he made a list of things to note. There was Smith, of course. And her father, the Marquess of Stallworth. Should he learn about other men with whom her mother had been involved? And what of the man bidding against them in the auction last night?

He didn't see how any of the pieces fit together.

Scratching his chin, he began to shave, the smooth rhythm of the blade calming his churning thoughts.

Surely there were connections he wasn't seeing, but how to find them? Whom did he ask?

He set down the straight razor as he considered. The easiest person to ask would be Smith himself.

Could he bait the man into some sort of trap and capture him?

He began shaving again. How might he get the man to show himself? Then he smiled.

He had the very thing Smith wanted—the diamond necklace. Could he use that to lure Smith somehow?

Nick started down to the breakfast room, prepared to wait for Aubrey, but in less than a quarter hour she appeared.

"You woke early as well?" she asked.

He nodded. He'd been in the habit of late and besides, his mind was too busy this morning, but at the sight of her in the dress she'd worn yesterday, he smiled. "Good morning."

"Good morning." A blush infused her cheeks as she looked down at her dress.

"I'll dispatch the footmen at once." He knew he'd promised to retrieve the projects that she wished to finish, but he was more concerned about her own wardrobe. She needed more than a single gown.

"Thank you," she answered as she crossed the room toward him. "But I won't need the gowns until after our meeting."

He reached for her hand, pulling her closer. "I didn't mean for just your work, I meant for your personal items."

The blush deepened. "You really intend for me to stay here? For how long?"

He didn't say *forever*. Instead, he laced his fingers through hers. "Until the danger has passed, at least."

She let out a long breath. "Thank you for that but..." He watched her nip at her lip, her face turning toward the side. "I have to ask..."

"Ask what?"

"Well." She pulled her fingers from his, then clasped them together. "What is it you wish in return?"

His brow furrowed. "Return?"

She drew in a deep, trembling breath. "Even my mother sold my legacy when she thought I wasn't pretty enough to make a decent match. Everyone wants something."

He winced, his heart going out to her. Last night, she'd said it wasn't a competition for worst childhood. But the idea that her mother had let Aubrey know she wasn't enough... And he'd contributed to that feeling, allowing his own friends to tease her for her crush on him. What a fool he'd been. "I don't want anything. At least nothing that you don't wish to willingly give. That's what friends do for one another."

She shook her head. "Friends? Is that what we are?"

"We were once before."

A small smile played at her lips as she looked at him again. "I do have a wonderful friend. Emily. And she does give to me out of the kindness of her heart. But I've never had a friend who was male before. And truth be told, if I'd realized we were only friends, I don't think I should have allowed you to kiss me last night."

He chuckled low and deep as he reached for her waist, pulling her close. "Perhaps we are a bit more than friends."

Her fingers fluttered up toward his chest, looking like the delicate wings of a bird, and she rested her palms against him.

"But..." He leaned down, brushing his nose across hers. "I promise we are not bartering for help here."

"Thank you," she said, sliding her hands over him. "I appreciate your generosity."

"Now," he said, pulling back enough to look down at her. "Tell me you have other gowns besides those padded ones."

"What does it matter?" she said, arching her brows. "Friend."

He nearly crowed with triumph. Did she rebel at the idea of them only being friends? "Even as your friend, I can appreciate your beauty."

He'd like to say more. How she stole his breath. How he couldn't believe he'd not noticed all those years ago the beauty she'd become.

"I might have a gown or two, and it would be nice to wear one of them to your solicitor today so as not to be in the same clothing I wore to the auction last night."

He crossed the room and pulled the cord, summoning a servant. "Make a list of the items you want and I'll see them brought here within the hour."

Her eyes widened as she gave a nod. "Thank you."

"Have a seat. I'll fetch the quill and paper myself."

He was glad she'd been a bit miffed. He didn't want to be just friends either. But first, he'd help her solve her mystery.

————

THE CARRIAGE RIDE to the solicitor passed in companionable silence.

She'd changed her gown, a floaty muslin frock skimming down her body. She'd seen Nick's gaze linger over her curves, her own body heating in response.

Friends.

The idea was ridiculous.

More was frightening, she could acknowledge that. But her feelings for him had always been far greater than that of friendship, and once again, she was being firmly placed in the category of friend.

He was a duke, she chastised herself. It wasn't as though he'd marry her. And honestly, he did her a great service by not asking her to be his mistress when he clearly wanted more from her.

She understood all of that.

But she had been rejected by him as a girl and the idea of being cast aside by him again made her ache.

Her fingers brushed through the loose curls that cascaded over one shoulder, her mouth pressing into a firm line. She'd be fortunate to leave Nick's company with her virginity still intact. Not only would he keep her safe, something she'd not been able to do on her own, he'd promise to see her placed in such a way as to care for herself.

For a woman who'd sworn independence, it was an odd feeling to be so dependent on a man. And, in her heart of hearts, to wish for more from him.

She'd fallen asleep last night to dreams of Nick. She'd fantasized about being in his bed and in his life. Not just as a friend or a passing fancy but as his partner.

Which was absurd.

Even if she'd have him—which she'd sworn never to open herself up like that—he'd never choose a woman like her. She was a seamstress and a bastard, no matter her lineage.

He was a duke who could have any woman he wanted. He'd never choose her. Even if by some miracle he did wish to make their relationship more serious, his friends had been so cruel when they'd been young—and that's exactly what would happen again

The carriage came to a stop and Nick helped her out, placing her arm in the crook of his elbow as they walked into the small office.

The solicitor stood waiting for their arrival, a smile on his face as he gave her a nod. "Madame Beauchamp. A pleasure to see you again."

"And you, Mister Hanson."

He gestured for them to enter his office and Nick helped her into one of the two waiting chairs on the near side of the desk.

Nick took the other and Mr. Hanson circled about the desk. "So, we're here to discuss the purchase of the Rivermore Diamond."

"No," Nick said with a quick shake of his head. "We're not."

Mr. Hanson, who'd been lifting his quill out of the inkwell, dropped it again. His eyebrows lifted as he looked from Nick to Aubrey. "We're not?"

"No. That's a discussion that can wait for another day, we've a more pressing matter to attend."

"Very well," Mr. Hanson said, carefully schooling his features into a polite mask once again. "What matter would you like address?"

"The sale of Madame Beauchamp's dress shop."

"To Madame Beauchamp?"

"No, to a one Mister John Smith. He's recently purchased the property. I'd like to know who he is and what motive he might have for the purchase."

Mr. Hanson assessed her again and Aubrey felt her cheeks flare with heat. She'd brought a great deal of trouble to Nick's door. And though she'd tried to keep him out of it, he'd become embroiled in her problems nonetheless.

"The more information you give me, the more targeted and thorough my research can be."

Nick looked at her and she gave a quick nod of agreement before Nick shared all that he knew of her situation to date. By the time he'd finished, her head hung low.

"Have you considered removing Madame Beauchamp from London?" Mr. Hanson asked.

Nick gave her a sidelong glance. "It's a good suggestion."

"My business," she cried, turning to Nick. "I could never."

He reached for her hand then. "You could start another."

"You don't understand." Her reputation was part of what kept her clients coming back. "I had years apprenticing and several more working hard to establish myself and expand my clientele. I'd lose so many customers."

"And Lord Stallworth, has anyone spoken to him?"

Her breath caught. She'd tried at the ball. "I could never just arrive at his home and ask to be seen."

"Why not?" Nick asked, his brows rising up.

"Because," she said, about to explain that seamstresses weren't just given audiences to bachelor marquesses. But dukes…

Nick's eyes gleamed as he looked back at her, clearly thinking the same thing. "What would you suggest we ask him, Mister Hanson?"

"The origins of the necklace, of course. His reason for gifting the jewel in the first place. And any recent inquiries into the piece would be a good start."

Nick nodded. "Anything else?"

"That's all I can think of for now. In the meantime, I'll begin researching this John Smith. He surely needed to have an address and some way to have raised the money for the shop and the coin he gave Madame Beauchamp."

Nick rose and she followed, Mr. Hanson getting up as well. "How long do you expect your inquiries to take?"

"A few days." Mr. Hanson's gaze flicked to Aubrey again. "In the meantime, consider my suggestion to leave the city. With His Grace's protection, you could surely start a new business in another location in England."

Aubrey gave a tight nod.

Much as she hated to admit it, there was wisdom in the words. She'd accepted Mr. Smith's offer because she hadn't had much choice, but also because she'd hoped to find some answers for her future.

But that future seemed to be spinning further and further from her control.

CHAPTER TEN

LATER THAT MORNING they stood in front of the stately entrance to the Marquess of Stallworth's home.

Aubrey's hand tightened on his arm as Nick knocked for the second time. It was early, just after eleven, but usually servants were up and about long before that hour, even if the lord was not.

"Are you sure we should be doing this?" Aubrey whispered, turning her head closer to his shoulder. "What if he won't see me?"

"He'll see you," Nick growled, his back growing straighter at the idea as every protective instinct he had kicked in at once. Aubrey had suffered enough at this man's hands. He'd not hurt her today, not if Nick could help it.

He raised his hand to clap the knocker a third time when the door finally opened. An ancient-looking butler appeared in the doorway, his hazy eyes squinting at Nick. "May I help you?"

"The Duke of Wingate and Madame Beauchamp are here to see the Marquess of Stallworth," Nick barked back, already irritated for being kept waiting and for the worry that had caused Aubrey.

Aubrey looked up at him as her brows rose. "You sound very dukely when you talk like that."

The muscles in his arms tightened as he pulled her a touch closer. "You get the full weight of my dukeliness on your side this morning."

He felt her relax. "Thank you."

The butler's head turned partially toward them and Nick would have wagered money that while the man's sight wasn't that good, his hearing was excellent. Not that they'd said much, but it was enough to give the butler a whiff that there might be trouble.

He showed them into a sitting room. "His lordship has not yet risen for the day. It might be better if you came back—"

"We'll wait," Nick answered before the man could finish.

The butler gave a curt nod before he disappeared.

"Shall we sit?" Nick asked. "I don't think refreshments are going to be served, and we might be here a while."

Aubrey gave him a tense smile. "I'm too nervous to sit, I think."

He nodded. "We'll do circles about the room, then. How does that sound?"

They started walking, a silence settling between them for a lap or two before Aubrey looked over at him. "I'm glad you're here."

"My pleasure."

"I'm grateful for everything. I truly am. But I've been picturing this moment since I was a small child, and now that's its finally come, I can't picture anyone I'd rather have next to me than you."

His heart swelled to hear the words.

He knew she wished for independence, so to also know that she needed him was gratifying to say the least.

"I'm glad to be here too. I've told you already, but I'll always support you."

Her mouth twitched down, a momentary frown creasing her forehead before the look was gone again.

Did she not want his offer of support? Did she worry that he'd disappear from her life again like he'd done when he was a teenager? Allow his friends to tease her?

He covered her hand with his. He was a man now, one who would protect her no matter the personal cost.

That, he could promise.

The door opened, and Nick turned his head, expecting to see the butler. Instead, the Marquess of Stallworth stood in the doorway, his expression firm but unreadable. "Your Grace. Madame." He executed a stiff bow.

"My lord," Aubrey murmured, bobbing into a curtsey, her voice trembling as she spoke.

He inclined his head.

"Shall we sit?" the marquess asked, gesturing toward the pair of settees near the fire.

"Let's." Nick led Aubrey to the seat as the marquess settled across from them.

"I know why you're here," the marquess said, his gaze settling on Aubrey. "I'm surprised you haven't come sooner."

Her lips parted. "You know who I am?"

"Of course," he answered, looking into the fire. "Just as I know His Grace purchased the diamond your mother sold."

Nick's brows lifted. Had the marquess been following the diamond, Aubrey, or both?

"Then you know I wasn't the only potential buyer."

"You were nearly outbid," the marquess answered.

Nick's gaze narrowed. Had the marquess been there? Sent a representative? Why? "You were watching the auction closely."

"The piece of family jewelry I had given my daughter was being auctioned off once again. I wanted to make certain it didn't fall into the wrong hands."

Like John Smith's hands? But Nick didn't ask that out loud. Not yet.

"Why did you give me that stone?" Aubrey asked, her voice still shaky.

The marquess hesitated. "It was my mother's. And her mother's before that. She didn't have any daughters, so she gave it to me, but it was meant to follow the female line."

Aubrey blinked as she looked at Nick and then back at her father. "But I'm not your line. Not really."

The marquess shook his head. "You're the closest thing I've got."

75

So the piece was a family heirloom but not a Stallworth heirloom. Interesting.

"If you feel that way," Aubrey said, just above a whisper, "why haven't we met before?"

The marquess grimaced. "I'm no good. That's why."

Aubrey let out a rush of breath. "That's hardly a reason."

Nick hid a smile, glad she was finding her feistier side in this conversation.

The marquess's jaw hardened. "It's reason enough."

"Has anyone else asked you about the stone?" Nick asked, making certain they covered all the necessary topics.

But the marquess's face went from stony to black. "Who else would ask me? I gave away the necklace years ago."

"One and twenty," Aubrey clarified, her jaw taking the same angle as her father's.

"Yes," the marquess answered. "Precisely. It's been a long time."

"And just to be clear"—she stood, her blue eyes glacial—"you didn't think I needed any help during that time. Not even when my mother died?"

———

AUBREY'S FEAR was quickly being replaced with anger. Good, old-fashioned irritation stiffened her limbs and raised up her chin until she was glaring down at the man. She might have been less angry if he'd said that he didn't want anything to do with a bastard child or that he'd forgotten she even existed.

But to have left her with her mother, the woman who'd declared her too ugly for a real future, or to have denied her his company when the only parent she'd ever known, bad or not, had died and left her completely alone in the world...

Had she made mistakes? Most certainly. She'd made a great many in the last week alone. But she was doing the best she could when she only ever relied on herself.

"She'd prepared you by supplying you with a trade."

"She sold my inheritance to support her own lavish life and condemned me to near poverty."

The marquess, her father, had the good grace to wince. "She had her faults."

"As do I," she said, letting out a long breath. Then she looked back at Nick. He gave her the smallest nod of approval. "But I suppose we need not talk about any of them. We're here to discuss the diamond."

Stallworth's brow crinkled. "Why? It's in your possession."

"It's in His Grace's possession." Aubrey clarified.

Nick stood next to her. "And someone is working very hard to relieve me of the piece."

Stallworth sucked in a breath as he looked at them both. "Who?"

"That," Nick said and reached for her hand, tucking it in his arm, "is what we're trying to find out."

Her fingers held his arm as her insides warmed at the touch. She'd already thanked him for being here, but another wave of gratitude washed over her. How would she have faced her father without him?

"So I'd like to repeat the question. Has anyone come to you about the necklace?"

"Not specifically," Stallworth answered, but he looked away when he said the words and she knew the man was lying. Why?

"Did anyone vaguely ask about the Rivermore?" Aubrey's other hand came to Nick's arm as well. Touching him brought her strength

"No." The marquess finally rose. "No one has asked. Now, if you'll excuse me, I have a schedule to keep."

The words jolted through her. She wasn't sure what she'd expected, but she shouldn't be surprised by such a dismissal.

She started to turn, but Nick didn't move, he stood tall and straight next to her, looking at her father with an unwavering gaze that would surely make any man shrink. In this moment, she wanted to kiss Nick again.

But he didn't glance her way now. Instead, he kept his gaze trained on her father. "Are you sure you wish to send us away so soon? It's unwise to do so to either of us for various reasons."

"Unwise?" Her father's chin rose another notch.

Nick drew in a deep breath, expanding his chest. "I'll let you decide why at your leisure. Madame Beauchamp, are you ready?"

"I am," she answered as she squeezed his arm again.

Without another word, he marched toward the front door, but as they exited, he placed a hand over both of hers, still tucked in his arm.

"I'm sorry he wasn't more receptive," he murmured as they made their way down the stairs.

"It's not your fault," she answered, shaking away the hurt. "I didn't expect much."

"I know, but still." He helped her into the carriage. "He could have at least helped you with some tidbit of information."

"All I can say is that I am now glad that you intercepted me at the ball. I couldn't have done any of this without you." She meant the words and it was far more than she'd ever normally admit.

He settled, not across from her, but next to her. "I'm glad that you're glad. And what's more, I'm working out a plan, but the details are a bit vague."

She gasped. "You are? What is it?"

He scratched his jaw. "I could hold another auction. See if I can get John Smith to attend now that he can't use you."

Aubrey leaned closer, excitement coursing through her body. "Of course, the necklace can be bait. What if I went back to my shop? He'd come and then I could tell him that—"

But she didn't have a chance to finish. In a heartbeat she was off the seat and moving through the air and nearly as suddenly she was in Nick's lap, his powerful thighs underneath her soft bottom.

"The necklace can be bait. You cannot."

"But he might not attend. He didn't the first time," she reasoned.

"Then we'll come up with another plan."

She opened her mouth to ask him what that might be, but before the words were out, his lips locked on hers. And then she was lost.

Even as his mouth claimed hers, he crushed her body to his chest, her softer curves molding to the hard planes of his body. She let out a whimper of need, and he responded by sliding one of his hands from the small of her back, up her torso, until he reached her breast.

When he cupped the weight of it in his palm, his finger flicking over the nipple, she arched into the touch.

She was in heaven. And all her objections were momentarily forgotten.

CHAPTER ELEVEN

NICK GROANED as her nipple puckered under his thumb, her body molded to his.

Aubrey wanted him as much as he wanted her. She made the loveliest little whimpering sound as he massaged the stiff peak again.

Damn, but he wanted to hear her moan out her pleasure.

He couldn't take her maidenhead. There was no promise between them and he cared far too much to ever leave her vulnerable like that, but that didn't mean that he couldn't bring her pleasure.

The idea of watching her face, hearing her moans, made him swell with desire and he made some guttural response as he settled her more deeply into his lap, pushing her back into his arm so that she half lay across him.

She went without protest, without even the slightest bit of resistance.

Last night, he'd felt her excitement, yes. But there had been a hesitation too that was gone today.

He'd gained some measure of trust and the idea of it was as intoxicating as the fullness of her breast in his palm.

"Do you like that?" he asked, leaning down to kiss her again.

Her feet lifted off the floor, stretching out on the bench as she arched into his continued adoration of her right breast.

Of course, the left deserved the same. He shifted, filling his hand with the other, giving her second nipple the same attention as the first. She arched against his hand, the slender column of her neck more exposed as he tipped her back, which meant that he trailed a liberal amount of kisses down its length.

She'd once again chosen a higher neckline. Likely wise, considering the hour of the day and the tasks they'd had to complete. But in this moment, he'd have given half his fortune to have her chest and the tops of her breasts exposed. He'd like to taste every inch of her, explore her skin with his hands and mouth.

He could spend days, years in the pursuit, tasting every inch of her. His hand swooped back down to her tiny waist and then over the flare of her hip, her curves making the desire surging inside him rise to a frenzy.

But she cried out a protest, her back still arched, and he knew she'd wanted his touch back on her breasts.

He smiled with male satisfaction. Nothing made a man happier, at least not this man, than pleasing a woman. But as his hand was rather enjoying the journey it was taking over her hip and down her leg, he dropped his mouth to her still-covered nipple and sucked.

Her gasping cry was all the satisfaction he needed as her fingers threaded into his hair, pulling him closer.

He reached the hem of her muslin gown and wrapped his fingers around her slender ankle for a moment before he started the journey back up her leg, this time under her skirts rather than on top of them.

He felt her shiver of pleasure and smiled as he turned his attention to the other nipple. Fair was fair.

But when he reached the ribbon that tied her stocking and moved past it so that his fingers met with the bare skin of her thigh, they moaned in unison. Her skin felt divine. So velvety, and he brushed his hand along the smooth softness, just enjoying the feel. But her legs naturally parted, inviting him higher, and who was he to refuse such an invitation?

He kept his touch light. This was a woman who had no experience. He needed to woo her into pleasure, though she'd been a very obliging student today.

As his fingers brushed over the silky hair at the juncture of her legs, the pad of his middle finger meeting the soft folds of her sex, she gasped and then moaned, pulling on his hair even harder.

He nearly chuckled out loud as he repeated the touch again and then a third time, always light, leaving her wanting more.

"Nick," she begged, tugging on the strands again. "Please. I need..." She didn't finish but she didn't have to. He knew exactly what she needed, and with that, he increased the pressure, circling her bud of pleasure as she pushed into his hand, clearly wanting more.

"Oh, Nick," she breathed. "I need...I..."

He loved his name on her lips like that. His cock was near bursting, not that he'd get any satisfaction now. But touching her like this, feeling her, hearing her, it was more than worth it. "I know, love. I know just what you need and I'll give you everything you want. I promise."

"Everything?"

"Everything." And then he moved even faster, her body so tight under his, he knew that she was close to the end.

She moaned again, her head thrashing back and forth before she let out a final cry, her body spasming in his arms before her body loosened, her limbs still trembling as she melted into him.

He let out a low groan, his head coming to her chest as he tried to catch his breath. There was so much he wanted to say and do. Instead, he smiled into her dress.

Slowly, her hands relaxed in his hair, her body soft and warm in his arms. "That was..."

"Magical."

She laughed softly. "Yes."

"I'm beyond honored that you allowed me to touch you like that." He lifted his head to look down into the soft blue of her eyes.

"I..." She looked back at him. "I trust you."

She didn't need to say more. He understood. He kissed her as the carriage made a quick turn. Lifting his head, he flicked open the curtain. They were nearly at his estate. Damn. He didn't want to leave the intimate little moment they'd created.

"Thank you for your trust," he said as he pulled her to sitting and began attempting to repair her state of dishabille.

She hesitated for a moment, her eyes darting from one side of the carriage to the other. "Perhaps," she started, her tongue darting out to lick her lips. "Perhaps you could show me how to do the same for you."

His mouth parted in surprise. How could he say no to such an offer as that?

———

SOMETHING INSIDE AUBREY HAD SHIFTED. She still didn't intend to marry. She'd spent most of her life attempting to learn to care for herself as the people around her failed her. But she did know that Nick was one of the few people who had truly helped her.

And she'd never wanted any man the way she did him.

And when he'd kissed her in the carriage, she'd made a decision. This was her chance to experience what she might never have the opportunity to feel again...passion.

He had not disappointed.

Never had her body been more alive than it had been in his arms. But she didn't want to just feel her own passion, she wanted to experience his as well.

He lifted her off his lap as quickly as she'd landed in it. In a blink, he was out of the carriage, half lifting her out too, and then, with his arm about her waist, he was guiding her inside, through the kitchen, and up the back stairs to a private sitting room in the back of the house.

More simply furnished and far more intimate than the one in the front had been, the room's fire crackled merrily in the hearth as he sat on the settee, pulling her into his lap once again.

She giggled, half from the breathless journey and half from nervousness, as her body melted into his.

And when his lips found hers, she forgot she was frightened as his tongue plundered her mouth.

"Aubrey," he finally whispered against her lips. "You feel so good, love." His hand traced her behind, giving the roundness a squeeze as their hips moved closer. Her legs naturally settled on either side of his, their nether regions coming together in a way that made her gasp in delight again.

Her skirts kept her from truly feeling him, but the bulge in his breeches still managed to cause the ache inside her to begin building again.

Dear Lord, what had this man done to her? He'd turned her into some wanton creature. Which nearly made her laugh. That had always been his specialty.

But rather than be hurt or worried that she was just another passing fancy, which she likely was, she was grateful.

No matter when he left her life, she knew for certain he'd leave it better. He'd save her from Smith, had helped her face her father.

It was with those thoughts that she slid her hand down the hard planes of his body to the falls of his breeches.

As a seamstress, she could work nearly any closure of clothing with one hand and she made quick work of all the buttons that held his breeches secure.

He growled out his appreciation. "You did that with impressive skill."

"Dexterous fingers," she returned as she pulled the fabric back and allowed his manhood to spring free.

And then she stopped.

Because he was just so...much.

He gave her that one-sided grin, the mischievous look that had irritated her in the past but now stole her breath. "Nick."

In answer, he reached for one of her hands and then wrapped her fingers about his girth, his hand over hers.

"It's far less complicated than your body," he murmured as he helped her work her hand up and down his length, his eyes half closed.

"And after watching your finish, I'm so ready I could practically burst."

Aubrey understood. Seeing his chest heave up and down, feeling the silky, thick length of him, her body was humming with want once again. She licked her lips. "Like this, we risk no pregnancy, correct?"

"Correct," he answered, his eyes opening again.

"So…" She kept working her hand along his length. "We could…do this again…without consequence?"

His hand over hers tightened. "There is a consequence for everything, but there would be no worry of a child."

A consequence for everything. That statement was true. It would be very difficult to let him go after this.

He'd been so much more than she'd ever expected.

But let him go? She'd have to. Because even if she didn't intend to remain single, which she did, he was a duke. He'd marry some woman of perfect lineage and unassailable virtue without a hint of scandal to her name.

A girl like the one she'd seen him with at the ball.

And her—she'd open her own shop if she was fortunate. Continue the charade of an older, widowed woman.

Which was why she'd enjoy these precious times when he belonged to her.

His body tightened under her, his hips straining up as his fist balled up at his sides.

With her free hand, she ran her fingers under his shirt, feeling the ridges of muscles along his abdomen, even as he helped her pump faster and faster.

She wanted more, she realized. She wished to see him without a shirt, feel his skin, taste his body.

She smiled to know that there would be a next time. For now, she'd focus on giving him the pleasure she'd been bestowed.

He gritted his teeth, his head titling back, the cords of his neck taut as his member pulsed in her hand.

Inexperienced as she was, she still knew that his finish was close, and her efforts redoubled to help him reach what he sought.

Her other hand flattened on his stomach, her fingertips pressing into his skin and the light spattering of hair.

And then he roared, his seed spilling from his manhood, his body tight with his finish. A satisfaction nearly as deep as her own climax washed over her to know that she'd given him that pleasure.

Warmth spread through her as she leaned over him to kiss him again.

His hand came up around her back, pulling her even more firmly to his chest as he kissed her over and over.

This moment was perfect. She didn't care what came next. She was happy now.

CHAPTER TWELVE

Aubrey's smile said it all. She looked so content as she pulled back, holding his gaze with her own.

Pleasing him had pleased her.

He pulled her back down, kissing her again as his fingers threaded into her hair. He'd like to pull out all the pins, take off every stitch of her clothing and touch her everywhere.

His finish hadn't diminished his desire for her in the least.

Which made the next thing he wished to say difficult. He kissed her again, wishing to delay the moment before he needed to say the words. "Aubrey."

"Yes?"

"What my solicitor said about you leaving the city. He's right."

She pulled back, blinking. "You want me to leave?"

He shook his head, taking her face in his hands. "Of course not."

"But you just said—"

"Sweetheart, I want you to be safe. There is a very large difference."

She nipped at her lip as she studied him. "I can't just leave, Nick. Not now."

"Why not?" he asked, sitting up and pulling her back into his lap.

"My business for one," she said as she sat stiffly in his embrace. "How would I fill all the orders I've taken?"

"Everything is here. You can take your supplies with you and send the completed dresses to your clients."

She shook her head, but she softened in his arms a bit. "There are fittings and consultations. It's not that simple, and leaving would ruin my business."

"As Hamilton said, you can start a new one if that's what you wish." He, for one, would like to add that she need not worry about the dresses at all. As a duchess, she'd not need to be a seamstress. But he wasn't ready to offer that future, simply because he doubted she wished to accept. He'd have to choose his moment very carefully. Aubrey was one of the women who prized her independence, and that was something he found he loved about her.

"If I wish?" She shook her head, her hands pushing against his shoulders. "I've tried explaining, I need my profession to sustain me."

He sighed. Did he point out that she had six thousand pounds and a diamond necklace? He kept silent. She didn't consider either asset to be hers, and while he loved her commitment to independence and ethics, he'd like to point out that the necklace was a gift willingly given and the money should be hers. Smith had attempted to kill her, in all likelihood. In his mind, attempted murder forfeited any claim the man had on the funds.

But he wondered if Aubrey would see the situation with the same light. Likely not. He'd attempted to tell her that he'd care for her, but on that front, he understood. Not very many people had actually done their parts to aid her in the past. He'd not believe him either if he were Aubrey.

"What would calm your fears in this regard?"

"Besides returning to my shop?"

Out of the question. "We've been over that. It's too risky." He spread his hands out on the small of her back, even the idea of her going back to her shop making him feel protective all over again. "I have a home in Bath. What if I escort you there myself, and while there, we purchase a property for your new shop? You could tell all your clients that the London air isn't agreeing with you, but you'll continue to serve them when they visit the healing waters."

She looked at him, her eyes widening. "It's not a bad plan, actually."

"So you'll consider it?"

"Perhaps…"

"Perhaps?" Why was this so difficult?

But her next words stole his breath. "Are you doing what your father did to my mother?"

He nearly choked on his own spit. "What?"

"He gave her a small bit of property. The gift made her happy at first, until she realized she was trapped far away from everything and everyone she knew."

He stood, still holding her waist. "Aubrey. Bath is a bustling place. I chose it specifically because you have access to all the same clients you have here, and many new ones I'm sure. I'm not tucking you away. I'm just keeping you from danger while I get rid of Smith in a way that enables you to continue your business."

She opened her mouth to answer, but her words were cut short by the sound of shattering glass.

Both of them looked to the door.

What had that been? Had a servant dropped a tray of glassware?

But the cry that followed was too delayed for broken glasses.

In a breath, Nick spun Aubrey behind him. "Stay here," he ordered, tugging up his breeches. "Hide behind the settee."

"Nick," she said, her voice high and tight. "Be careful."

"I will." He wrenched open the door, shutting it tightly before sprinting down the hall. It didn't take him long to find the disturbance.

In the entry, the window above his front door was broken and mangled, and a large stone lay on the floor amidst the glass, the marble where it landed cracked and broken.

"Your Grace," his housekeeper cried. "Who would do such a thing?"

He could think of someone.

Around the stone was a piece of twine and attached to that was a bit of parchment. Sifting through the glass, he grabbed the sheet, unfolding it to find a handwritten note. The handwriting was almost angry, the words slashing across the paper.

GIVE me the necklace and the woman. I won't ask twice.

HIS HAND TIGHTENED on the sheet. Smith.

The villain could ask a thousand times, the answer would be the same. He'd never give Smith the necklace. And Nick would die before he allowed the other man to touch one hair on Aubrey's head.

AUBREY DID AS NICK ASKED, staying behind the settee until the door opened again. She froze for a moment until she heard Nick's voice. "Aubrey?"

Without hesitation, she jumped up, running to his arms. "What happened?"

She saw his grimace a moment before he caught her in his embrace. "Everything's fine."

"That isn't what I asked," she said as she pressed her stomach to his, but then leaned her head back to look up into the depths of his green eyes.

His frown only deepened. "A rock came through the window in the entry."

She gasped. "What?"

He held her tightly, closing the door behind him. "I've got all the footmen on guard. You needn't worry."

Needn't worry? Her arms snaked about his neck. Someone—no, not someone, she knew who'd done this. "Smith?"

"Yes."

Her eyes fluttered closed. "I can't believe he'd be so bold."

He'd already attacked Nick's carriage. "The funny, interesting part—"

"Interesting?" she asked, looking up at Nick as he stared somewhere over her shoulder, clearly lost in thought.

"I thought he wanted the necklace and he was using you to get it," Nick whispered, as much to himself as her.

"Of course that's what's happening." What else would it be?

"Aubrey," he said, spreading his hands protectively over her back. "I'll not allow him to hurt you. Promise me that you'll let me protect you."

His words frightened her a bit. What was his new concern? She let out a breath. She had done a fair bit of fighting his suggestions.

Was she being a fool? Likely yes. Her independence had been her armor for a very long time. But without Nick's help this time, she'd be so much worse off, of that she was certain. "I will. I promise."

"Good," he answered with a nod but didn't loosen his grip.

"Are we leaving for Bath?" She'd not wished to go, but after the incident that had just happened, she had to think of Nick as well. She was bringing danger to his door by staying in his home.

He looked at her then, his eyes focusing in on her face. And then he kissed her, long and hard in a way that stole the air from her lungs and the reason from her mind. When he finally lifted his head, he gave it a shake. "Not yet."

That surprised her. Wasn't that what they'd just been discussing? "What then?"

He grimaced as he finally let her go, reaching into his breast pocket and pulling out a piece of parchment.

After handing her the sheet, she flipped it open, reading the words. "He can't mean me?"

"He does."

"But…" She looked down at the words again. "He tried to kill me yesterday."

Nick blinked, taking the sheet from her hand. "Or he tried to kill me."

She gasped. "What do you mean?"

His hands slid about her again. "I bought the necklace and then I had you in my carriage. Perhaps he was firing to kill me and take both you and the jewel."

"But why would he want me? He blackmailed me. He—"

"He bought your shop," Nick said, searching her face again. "He gave you an extravagant amount of money. He..." Nick shook his head. "Did he want both you and the necklace?"

"That makes no sense. Why wouldn't he have spent time with me? Helped me with the purchase?"

"I don't know, but he wouldn't ask for you if all he wanted was the jewel."

Fear shivered down her spine. "What does that mean?"

"It means that I'm not letting you out of my sight." He held her waist in his large hands. "And we won't travel, which would make you vulnerable."

A smile tugged at her lips. "Does that mean that for once in this process, I was a little bit right?"

He smiled too. "I suppose it does, though we can't go to your shop. You understand, don't you?"

She did. What was more, she appreciated all his efforts so much. Someone had attacked his home and yet here he stood, holding her close and more committed to her safety than ever.

In her entire life, no one had ever done so much for her, been so devoted to her well-being.

It was more than she'd ever dreamed of and she found herself lifting up on tiptoe to press her mouth to his. The kiss was soft but it lingered.

And then another press of their mouths lasted even longer.

By the time she pulled back, they were both panting for breath.

His mouth swooped back down, claiming her lips in a kiss that went from exciting to molten as she threaded her fingers up into his hair.

Somehow tonight, nearly every barrier she normally kept between herself and the world had come crashing down.

She was open to him in ways she'd never imagined, and her body hummed with the joy of it.

As they kissed, his fingers began working down the delicate buttons at the back of her gown.

She ought to stop him. Taking off her clothing made her even more vulnerable and while she wished to touch him, she had to be careful not to allow things to go too far.

But she didn't want to hold back. Not from him. Not anymore...

CHAPTER THIRTEEN

NICK FELT THE DRESS GIVE, triumph swelling inside him.

Working the delicate buttons of her sleeves, he removed the bodice, then her skirts.

"I..." she started as he rose with the delicate fabric in hand.

He could see the vulnerability shining in her eyes. Holding her chin, he kissed her lips again. "I'll keep you safe."

He meant from Smith, but he also meant she was safe in his arms. He had the control to give her what she needed without compromising the parameters she'd set forth. No risk of pregnancy.

She melted into him again as he tugged at the strings of her short corset, freeing her of another piece of clothing.

Nick couldn't help but grin as her hands began tugging at his coat and then his shirt.

He obliged her by shrugging off the jacket and pulling the shirt over his head. Then her bare arms wrapped around his back, the skin-to-skin contact making him rumble with even more need as he claimed her mouth over and over.

His attempts to remove her clothing grew more frantic and less effective as he slid his other hand down over her chemise, cupping her breast in his hand. He wanted the clothing gone, to kiss her nipple and really taste her.

She arched into his touch, groaning, and he finally managed to loosen the strings of her petticoat, the mass of fabric dropping to the floor.

And then he grabbed the hem of the chemise, pulling it up and over her head so that she stood before him in nothing but stockings and slippers.

The breath hissed from his lungs. Whatever he'd imagined, dreamed, the reality was so much better.

Her breasts sat high and round, each easily filling his palm, while her chest tapered to a small waist and flat stomach. But her hips flared out, adding the sort of shape that a man could only dream of.

He hooked her waist again, pulling her close before lifting her up, wrapping his arms under her behind to carry her the short distance back to the settee.

Once there, he laid her down, kissing her mouth one more time before he began to blaze a trail along her neck to her shoulder and then down her chest.

He stopped, providing ample attention to each of her rosy breasts, the nipples so tight that he couldn't help but kiss each of them again.

One silky calf wrapped about his back, the stocking sliding along his skin.

And that's when he took a moment to appreciate that he had this woman near naked in his arms.

He'd never take that for granted. Not ever.

It was that thought that finally coerced him into continuing his exploration down her belly and then lower.

He kissed along one of her hips, worshiping the shape of it before he cut across her legs, working toward the V at her apex.

As he got closer, her felt her shiver, but he didn't hesitate as he kissed in the crease of her leg and then closer until he finally brushed his lips over her soft folds.

Her cry was all the encouragement he needed as he kissed her again, the heady perfume of her arousal encouraging him to flick out his tongue for a quick stoke along her seam.

"Nick," she gasped, her fingers digging into his hair. "Oh my lord, that is…"

He nearly chuckled but held it in as he flicked his tongue out again. She grew wetter by the second, her fingers threading into his hair as he went from teasing to serious, stroking her in a way that he knew would bring her the satisfaction she sought.

Her body moved with his, riding the pleasure closer and closer to her peak until he gently inserted a finger into her channel. Her body clamped about him and then she broke apart, crying out his name as her pleasure crested.

He roared up, his legs still between hers on the settee, torso hovering above hers as he drank in the sight of her from her passion-glazed eyes to the rosy hue of her flushed breasts. The way her chest heaved from the desire.

Aubrey was his. She'd never belong to anyone else.

Sinking back down, he ran his fingers from her cheek down her arm and across her hip, tracing her like a path that he was mapping. Memorizing.

Her arms threaded about his neck, her lips finding his. "That was…"

He kissed her rather than filling in the single word that came to mind…*transformative*. Perhaps that wasn't completely true.

He'd already known that Aubrey belonged with him, but now, he was deep down in his gut certain.

Any doubts or worries that he held had been burned away by their passion.

Without a word, he sifted through their clothing and found his shirt. Crossing back to her, he pulled the garment over her head.

"What are you doing?"

"Taking you upstairs," he answered, lifting her into his arms.

"In just a shirt and stockings?" she yelped.

"You're wearing slippers too."

Her mouth pressed into a line even as her arms came about his neck. "Yes. I know that, thank you."

He started out the door but her grip tightened. He stopped again. "What's wrong?"

"What if someone sees me?"

"My staff will stay well out of our way," he answered, continuing on again. He understood her hesitation. But he had a powerful need to hold her in his bed and he knew very well they'd encounter no one in his halls.

"Your staff," she repeated, her fingertips digging into the skin of his neck.

He could feel the tension returning to her body. "I told you. You need not worry. No one will see us."

"Because you're a duke," she answered, visibly swallowing.

He started up the back stairs, moving quickly. Though he knew they were alone, he'd much rather have this conversation with her safely tucked in the covers of his bed. "That's right."

She didn't say another word, but her silence only seemed to add to the tension. What had just happened?

———

Nick's words had been an instant reminder to Aubrey. He was a duke. Dukes did not live happily ever after with seamstresses. And she had better remember that as she felt more and more of her guards falling away.

If she weren't careful, she was bound to be hurt.

Though it might be too late already.

Then she chastised herself. She didn't wish for a future with this man or any man.

He pushed open a door, where a small fire lit the dark room. Even in the dim light she could see the room was large, an enormous bed seeming to fill one wall.

He kicked the door closed behind him, ignoring the crash as he started for the bed.

"But…" She licked her lips. "I have my own room, remember."

"This one is more comfortable."

She tried again, suddenly nervous. "What about my clothes? We left them strewn about that sitting room." She wasn't afraid that he'd do something she wasn't comfortable with, more that in a moment of weakness, she'd allow him to do nearly anything.

The man had gotten under her skin.

"Someone will clean them up and return them to your room." He lay her down on the bed then, his body coming on top of hers, making her eyes flutter closed as the air whooshed from her lungs. What was it about his weight that was so wonderful?

"Someone?"

He began kissing a trail down her neck. "Is it strange for you? To be waited on?"

"Yes, I suppose it is." Though that was the least of her concerns at this very moment.

More concerning was that he'd settled between her thighs with the bulge in his breeches pressed into her womanhood. Once again, her body was responding to his in a way that made it hard to think.

"You'll get used to it."

She blinked several times as she tried to process those words. "Used to it?"

He stilled and then lifted up his chest, looking down at her. "Aubrey." He drew in a deep breath as he traced a finger down her nose. "I want you to be my wife."

She gasped, jumping several inches up and then falling back down because she was trapped by his body. "Wife?" she cried as she sank back into the soft bed.

His gaze narrowed. "I know you don't wish to wed."

"I don't," she said, as much for her own benefit as his. He couldn't mean it. He was different this time, she knew that. But different enough to marry her?

He grimaced. "You don't have to sound quite so certain. I think we're good for each other."

She drew in a steadying breath. "We are. But I'm not the woman for the dukedom."

"The dukedom can hang."

"Nick!"

"I'm serious. I thought never to marry, but a seamstress would serve my father right for being such—"

She didn't let him say more as she smacked his chest. "You want to marry to get back at your father?"

He had the decency to wince. "I didn't mean it like that."

"Really? Sounded that way to me." Her eyes filled with tears. There was no denying that he'd helped her so much the past several days. And she supposed she ought to be grateful he would marry her no matter the reasons.

But for a woman who'd felt like she'd never been able to trust anyone, to think that he'd only wished to hurt someone else, that it wasn't because of genuine feeling…

Did anyone ever just want her?

"Aubrey, is it not obvious that I would twist myself into knots to give you what you need? You said you trusted me."

Did he sound hurt? How did he get to be hurt? "I do trust you. No one has ever helped me so much."

"Then how can you not know that my feelings are genuine?"

She shook her head. His words about his father had cast some shadow of doubt when she already had so many. She'd made her rules about the future for a reason. She couldn't risk being hurt again by someone who was supposed to love her. "I need to think."

He rolled away, scraping his hands through his hair. "You need to think?"

"Yes. Think." And then she jumped from the bed and ran. At least she still wore her slippers. They padded softly on the thick carpet as she fled.

CHAPTER FOURTEEN

How HAD that gone so terribly wrong?

Nick sat on the bed as the clock ticked, counting the seconds or the hours, he couldn't be certain.

How was he that unlovable?

Handsome. Rich. Titled. He'd literally gone in and rescued her, and still she didn't want him.

His heart throbbed painfully in his chest.

His parents hadn't loved him and neither would the woman he wished to make his wife.

But the more time that passed, the more his thoughts cleared. He hadn't meant to hurt her with his comment about his father.

And she'd been abandoned by so many.

Did she think that he didn't really love her? That he was only doing this to hurt his father? If he wanted to win Aubrey, that was not the way to do it.

Bloody hell. He'd messed up the whole thing.

It was just...telling her that he'd fallen completely in love made him so vulnerable. He'd been hiding behind that comment about his father. He could see that now.

Did he go to her room and tell her so?

THE DUKE WHO DARED

What time was it? He shook his head. It had to be the wee hours of the morning. He'd wait. Tell her the whole truth. He'd fallen in love. That being with her was all that mattered.

With that, he finally lay down.

But he only slept a few hours before he was up again. He bathed and dressed, making his way down to breakfast, though today, Aubrey did not join him.

He should have known. He'd hurt her last night.

As he sat eating, his butler appeared. "Your Grace."

Nick lifted his head. "Yes?"

"Mister Hanson is seeking an audience. He claims that he has information you'd like to know immediately."

He pushed back his chair. "Show him in to the front sitting room."

The butler gave a nod, disappearing again.

His breakfast could wait. If Mr. Hanson had come this early in the morning, he'd unearthed something important.

Leaving the breakfast room, he trotted down the stairs to the sitting room where he found Mr. Hanson standing near the front windows.

"Mister Hanson," Nick said, looking around the sitting room where he'd first kissed Aubrey. His chest tightened.

"Your Grace." His solicitor turned to face Nick, looking grim as he gave a quick nod.

"What have you learned?"

"A fair bit."

Nick's gut clenched.

"First, Mister Smith is really Mister Waters, his mother's surname."

"Waters?"

"That's right. She was surely named after the brothel she lived and worked in on the banks of the Thames."

"And he changed the name to Smith?"

"It's a clever choice. John Smith is an utterly forgettable name and hard to trace because there are so many."

"And why would he need a forgettable name?"

"He's a smuggler, as far as I can tell. He owns property on the docks and on a few ports up the coast."

"You're painting an excellent picture. Do you think he trades in jewels? Is that why he wants the necklace?"

"I don't know about what he smuggles."

"Then why did he go to Aubrey to obtain the necklace?"

"If I were to guess, it has something to do with the fact that they are related."

"Related?" The knots in his stomach twisted.

"Half-siblings. Different mothers but the same father."

His fists clenched. "Smith is also one of Stallworth's offspring?"

"That's right."

"Her brother," he whispered as the details began to click into place. No wonder he'd gone to Aubrey to get the necklace rather than just procuring the stone himself.

But that still didn't explain his true intentions. Did Smith want a relationship with her? Had he intended to actually give her the dress shop?

"Any chance you have addresses for the properties he owns?"

"I do." Mr. Hanson pulled out a slip of paper from his breast pocket.

Nick flipped open the sheet, reading the three addresses listed. "Thank you."

"Do you intend to visit him?" Mr. Hanson asked, his hands clasping behind his back.

"I can't think of any other way to find out his intentions." Nick tucked the sheet in his own pocket.

"Then I must insist on going with you."

"Why?"

Mr. Hanson frowned. "I saw your window as I entered the house. That's twice he's attacked you."

Nick grimaced. The man had a point. In fact, he might do well to have more than just the two of them. "I've got a few friends who like a bit of adventure. I'll ask them to join us as well."

Mr. Hanson gave a nod. "Excellent idea, Your Grace. Shall we?"

"Yes." But then he frowned. "But first, I need to write Madame Beauchamp a quick message. She'll want to know what you've learned."

"Of course." Mr. Hanson turned back toward the window. "I'll wait here."

Nick moved to the desk, and pulling out parchment and quill, began to explain all that he'd learned. They needed to talk, he knew that. But right now, his first priority was to do as he'd promised all along...keep Aubrey safe.

———

AUBREY WOKE LATE, the sun streaming in through the windows. That was the problem with crying one's self to sleep. It had taken an excessively long time and the sleep had been very interrupted after she'd finally managed to drift off.

A duke had proposed.

How could she be this upset? But the knot of sick dread twisted up her stomach still. Despite the fact that she'd told herself a hundred times she didn't want to wed, but Nick had always been the exception. The man who'd always held her attention and, if she was honest, her heart.

And when he'd asked, for a moment, she'd forgotten all her objections. This was the man she'd always wanted, and despite everything, he wanted her too.

Then he'd gone and tainted the entire offer. Was she just a way to hurt the man who'd neglected him as a child?

Despite the fact that his father was long dead, Aubrey understood perfectly how those old wounds could still ache. Still shape the future.

But she'd not be a tool for Nick. She couldn't. Aubrey would do better to spend her life alone than be a pawn in his plot for revenge.

But this time the words felt hollow and her heart brittle. Having someone to aid her, to trust... Her life had been richer since Nick had returned and if she gave that up, her world would be grey again.

That was what surprised her. She wanted to open her heart to him. She wanted to love and be loved.

But she didn't feel any closer to making that a reality, despite his marriage proposal.

A maid entered the room, giving her a bright smile. "You're up, my lady."

Aubrey nodded, not correcting the other woman. She wasn't a lady. Not even close.

But she rose from the bed. "Have I missed breakfast?"

"A tray will be delivered here to your room," the maid said with a curtsey. "And any additional provisions you need will be provided, of course."

Aubrey wasn't certain what she'd expected. Derision? Barely contained hostility? But the maid's open and friendly demeanor left her throat dry. Would the staff really treat her as a duchess?

"But I've also come to deliver a message."

"A message?" Her stomach dropped clear to her toes. "From whom?"

"His Grace," the maid said as she pulled a note from the pocket of her apron. "He wanted you to have this as soon as possible."

Aubrey took the paper with trembling fingers. "Thank you."

"Shall I stay to help you ready for the day?"

"That won't be necessary," she said, her voice barely rising above a whisper. She didn't wish for anyone to see her when she read this note.

What if he asked her to leave? What if he never wished to see her again? Her breath came out in shallow gasps, and the woman gave a quick bob and then left.

Her hands felt heavy as she slowly unfolded the sheet, her eyes already blurring.

But she blinked back the water as words jumped out at her.

BROTHER.

Gone to find him.

Keep my promise.

I'd never let anyone hurt you.

She shook her head, reading the entire missive again. He hadn't given up on her. This note was full of concern. Of promises. Of work he poured into her under the guise of keeping her safe.

But then other thoughts sifted through, rising to the surface. John Smith was her brother?

Which meant that her father had lied. Didn't it?

She rose, crossing the room to pull the silken cord hanging by the door. Was Nick in any danger? Should she find him?

How could she do that? Where had he gone to find her brother?

There was only one person she could think to ask—her father.

After pulling the cord, she spun and started for the wardrobe. It was time for some answers.

She'd need a bit of help. Crossing to the desk, she pulled out a quill. Hopefully, Emily could slip away from her mother long enough to attend this interview with Aubrey.

CHAPTER FIFTEEN

Nick pounded on the door of the stately London townhome for the third time. He knew Eric was inside.

Eric Henderson was one of his oldest friends. Technically, the man was now Viscount Shipley, but Nick would always think of Eric as a fourteen-year-old boy who climbed trees and teased girls.

As Lord Shipley, the man was a terrible rake, and Nick had no doubt that his friend had been up most of the night, his staff with him, but still. It was after ten in the morning. Surely someone in the house had risen.

"What in the bloody blazes is all that racket?"

A window above Nick slid open and a shirtless Eric hung his head out the window.

Behind Nick, a woman passing by made a gasping noise followed by a scandalized clucking of her tongue.

Nick smiled to himself. "Did I wake you?"

"You know damned well that you did."

His grin widened. "My sincere apologies, but I've got a situation that requires immediate assistance."

"A situation? Why didn't you say so? I'll be right down."

Nick stepped back. And that was why he'd come to Eric. The man was a true friend.

He returned to the carriage, prepared to wait, but less than a quarter hour later, Eric appeared, tossing open the carriage door. His chin held a heavy shadow, his eyes were bleary, but he wore two pistols at his belt and he carried a hunk of bread and a chunk of cheese.

"I'll be right by the time we arrive," he said as he settled in, taking a bite of the bread. "Just need to settle my stomach."

Nick shook his head, suppressing a chuckle. "But you don't even know how long it will take to get there."

"It doesn't matter. I'll be right. Are we dueling in the park?"

"Good God, no," Mr. Hanson chimed in. "I could never partake in such an adventure."

Nick understood. Dueling was illegal.

"Is Jacob in town?"

"No. Out in the country. His father…" Eric grimaced.

Nick didn't need to hear more. Three would have to suffice. "Well, in that case, we're conducting an investigation."

"Into…"

Nick scratched at his jaw. "Let me think. How best to share…"

"His Grace decided to help a woman who is being blackmailed," Mr. Hanson offered.

That was one way to put it. "Not just any woman. Aubrey Fairfield."

"Aubrey?" Eric cried, nearly dropping the cheese. "When did you reconnect with Aubrey?"

"He knows her?" Mr. Hanson asked, leaning forward.

"We all grew up together," Nick murmured.

"That does make more sense."

"Please, don't feel as though you need to answer the viscount's question," Eric muttered as he took another bite.

"Sorry, old friend." Nick gave a shake of his head. "I found Aubrey at a ball, of all places, pretending to be a debutante. She was there to meet her father, of whose identity you are surely aware."

"I am."

"She needed an escort to a jewel auction because, as far as we can now tell, she was being blackmailed by her half-brother, another one of Stallworth's bastards."

Eric took a bite of cheese. "And here I was thinking your life had grown boring."

That made Nick smile again. "I've missed you, old friend."

"And I you. Tell me, how does Aubrey fare despite the black-mailing?"

"She is so beautiful, you'd hardly recognize her," Nick answered, the awe creeping into his voice.

Eric's brows lifted. "Interesting."

As quickly as Nick could, he filled in the rest of the details, the carriage rumbling from respectable London toward the eastern docks.

"And so now we're doing what?"

"We"—Nick took in a deep breath—"are going to attempt to find Mr. Smith and ask him a few questions."

"Ah…" Eric nodded. "I understand."

"It might be dangerous."

Eric shrugged. "That's why I ate cheese."

"I beg your pardon?" Mr. Hanson asked, his gaze narrowing.

"It's my favorite." Eric shrugged, beginning to load his pistols. "If I do survive, I'd like to see Aubrey again."

Nick shook his head. "I'm not sure she'd like to see you. Or me. She is angry about the way we treated her in the past and not too happy about my choice of words in the present." He hoped that note helped her understand that he still had her best interests at heart.

"Not happy about the past?" Eric grunted, stuffing lead down the barrels. "Well, we'll have to live, then. There are some things I might need to set straight. And besides. I'm getting married, I think."

Nick's head whipped back. "Married?"

"Maybe." Eric shrugged, looking as unconcerned about marriage as he did about death. "I'll tell you all about it later. For now, let's find your criminal."

Nick pulled out two pistols of his own. He hoped this was just a conversation, but then again, violence seemed to erupt whenever John Smith was near.

———

AUBREY SAT in the hack just around the corner from Emily's family townhouse. She hadn't seen her friend since the night of the ball and she'd missed her.

Emily came rushing around the corner, looking quickly behind her before she hopped into the carriage.

"You were able to sneak away," Aubrey said as she leaned over to hug her friend.

"My mother thinks that I'm taking a repose, but I've only so much time," Emily replied, hugging Aubrey back. "And I've missed you. Where have you been?"

The carriage began to move and as quickly as Aubrey could, she told her friend all that had happened.

Emily gasped when Aubrey told her that Nick had proposed. "A duchess?"

Aubrey shook her head. "He said he wished to punish his father."

Emily's brows rose. "How do you punish a dead man?"

Aubrey didn't answer, but Emily's mother spent so much time controlling her daughter that Aubrey suspected if the countess were to die, Emily might marry a man her mother would most definitely not approve of out of spite alone.

"For me, that matters less than the fact that I would only be a means to an end."

Emily shook her head. "Forgive me, friend, but wouldn't your duke also be a means to an end for you?"

"How so?"

"You'd have the security you've always sought."

"But not the way I sought it."

Emily reached for her hands. "That is so often the case in life. The path is rarely what we thought it would be. The question is, do you arrive where you need to be?"

Aubrey frowned, considering those words. "I wished to be independent." Did she need that? That's the question Emily had asked. She thought she did. But then again, her desire for independence was, to a certain extent, a wish made out of fear.

She was afraid to give her heart to anyone.

And fear didn't make her strong at all. It made her weak.

She sucked in her breath as the hack rolled to a stop outside her father's home. She winced as she waited for the driver to open the door.

Emily reached for her hand and Aubrey gave the other woman's fingers a squeeze before the door opened.

Here she was again. She wished Nick were next to her.

She was glad Emily was here, but his strength had carried her through the last meeting with her father. Nick's strength had carried her through this entire mess.

Which brought her back to Emily's word. Besides independent, what she'd really wanted to be was...well, she wished to be whole. Not the broken girl who'd been teased mercilessly and not the woman that John Smith had been able to take advantage of so readily.

And allowing people like Emily, and even more so Nick, into her life had infused her with...strength. Hope. Joy.

She squared her shoulders as the front door opened. This time she didn't need to knock six times and that was encouraging too.

Lifting her skirts, she started up the stairs, nodding to the butler as she passed. Her father stood in the entry waiting. "You came back."

"I did."

His eyes held hers, much of the coldness that had filled them the last time gone. "I'm glad."

She started at the words. "Really? I'd have never guessed after my last visit."

Behind her, Emily's hand touched her shoulder.

"Forgive an old man for so many mistakes." He shook his head. "I was worried you were here for the same reason as Waters."

"Waters?"

"Smith," her father said as he gestured toward the sitting room. "A name I helped him make legitimate, I'm afraid."

Her feet halted. "What?"

"Please sit down, I'll tell you everything."

She did as her father instructed, Emily taking the seat next to her as introductions were made.

The marquess took the seat across from them, his gaze looking tired as he stared down at the hands he'd folded in his lap. "Waters sought me out about five years ago, much as you did." He lifted his chin, looking out the window. "I confess that in my elder years, I regret some of my choices as a younger man."

Aubrey swallowed as she listened. She didn't know what to say. She couldn't console him. It was neither her place nor his right.

"I should have..." He sighed. "I should have married. In fact, I should have married your mother."

She swallowed again, this time her throat burning. "It's a bit late for that sentiment."

"I would have made a terrible husband and father. Truly awful. But it would have been better..."

Aubrey could not look at him. His remorse did not help her with her current predicament. "Waters?"

"Yes." One of her father's hands lifted. "He came to me with an idea to make him a legitimate heir. "

She gasped. "But that's illegal."

He gave her a small smile. "I told you I'd make a terrible father."

"You were tempted because of your regrets," Emily supplied with a small smile. "I understand."

"I was. Thank you," he said, relief making his shoulders sag.

Aubrey looked at her friend, her eyes wide with surprise. Emily understood exactly what the marquess needed to hear.

"But it was a mistake and I knew almost from the beginning. The funds I gave him to set up a legitimate life, he mostly used to fund his criminal activities. He demanded more and more from me, leveraging my contacts to sell his goods."

"Goods?"

"Wine from France. Salt. Anything he can get his hands on and sell without paying tax. I tried to explain to him that if he were to become a marquess, he'd need to rebuild his life into one that appeared perfect. No hint of scandal. But he didn't listen."

"What happened next?" Aubrey asked.

His chin dropped once again. "His behavior became more and more erratic until…" The marquess drew in a sharp breath. "I cut him off. I told him that if I were going to make a child legitimate, it would not be him." The marquess's eyes wavered with uncertainty. "I told him it would be you."

Aubrey gasped. "But I can't inherit your title."

"I know that. But he's the son of a whore who grew up on the docks."

"He believed you." Aubrey began to understand. She was his competition for the marquess's wealth.

"Even if he didn't, he knew the bulk of my fortune now does not lie in my entailed property but in the collection of jewels my mother amassed. One of which I gifted to you upon your birth."

Aubrey's hands trembled as she smoothed out her skirts. "I see."

"And he also knows that I've willed all the pieces to you upon my death."

She gasped. "What?"

"I should have married your mother. You, beautiful girl, are every-thing that I should have grabbed with both hands and held on to."

The words reverberated through her, though she didn't know quite how to feel about them. She'd been an outcast her entire life. That legacy was part of her now. "I'm not asking that of you. I'm not asking you for anything except…"

"Except what?"

"Nick. The Duke of Wingate, he—"

"What's your relationship with the duke?"

"He proposed," Emily answered for her, and she shot her friend a look. That was another topic on which she hadn't entirely sorted her feelings.

"Did he?" The marquess looked very pleased. "How wonderful."

THE DUKE WHO DARED

"Regardless. He found an address for John Smith and he's gone to confront the man."

"Oh, His Grace shouldn't do that," the marquess answered. "Waters is dangerous."

"You should have told us that the last time," Aubrey said, her voice rising.

The marquess winced. "It's a delicate business, my relationship with my son. The dealings we'd had..."

Aubrey sighed. And she tried to think of what Emily might say. "I understand. But I need to find Waters, or Smith, now and help Nick."

The marquess nodded. "We'll go together."

She rose, trying to decide how to answer. "You want to come with me?"

"I would very much like to see you wed to His Grace. Not only would it continue my bloodline, but it would right so many of the wrongs. Not the least of which is that I was a fool. Waters is callously stupid and reckless. It brings me great joy to think one of my progeny has a solid head on her shoulders."

Aubrey's jaw tightened. She thought of all the mistakes she'd made throughout this process. But Nick...he'd kept her safe. Kept her on the right path.

She looked at Emily. No, Nick wasn't the path she'd planned, but he was taking her in the right direction. She could see clearly that her father regretted not marrying her mother. Would she feel the same about Nick if she let him go?

Her heart told her that she would.

CHAPTER SIXTEEN

Nᴉᴄᴋ's ᴄᴀʀʀɪᴀɢᴇ pulled to a stop near the warehouse address.

"He might not even be there," Mr. Hanson said as he parted the curtain to assess the street.

"Might not," Nick agreed. "How do we find out?"

"Knock on the front door?" Eric asked, craning his neck to have a look out the window. "I always like the direct approach. Gets things done quickly."

"As long as you're not killed," Hanson said, frowning at Eric. "Tell me. Do you have your affairs in order?"

Eric chuckled then. "We'll discuss them after we're done here."

Hanson shook his head as his serious gaze met Nick's. "He should wed. He needs an heir quickly if he lives his entire life like this."

Nick didn't comment. He'd lived like Eric not so long ago, which was as astounding as it was eye-opening. He didn't miss Eric's world a bit.

Aubrey was his future.

"I'm going to do a quick search of the back of the property and see if I can learn anything before we go banging on the front door."

Hanson shook his head. "I will."

"But..."

Hanson started for the door. "As your solicitor, I must insist." And then the man was out of the carriage and down the alley.

"He moves with an incredible silence," Eric said as he watched the other man disappear.

"Sobriety is the trick," Nick answered, raising his brows. "And since we're alone. Do tell me about your impending marriage."

Eric was a good man and a steadfast friend. But Nick had to wonder if marriage was wise at this time. Nick was ready to settle. Eric seemed far from it.

Nick shrugged. "My third cousin, the current Earl of Sanbridge, is dying."

"You're about to become the earl?" Nick sat up straighter.

Eric nodded. "In his most recent letter, he suggested that I marry his stepdaughter. Said she'd aid me in taking over the earldom."

"His stepdaughter?" Nick asked with a frown. "Why not one of his actual daughters?"

"Don't know." Eric shrugged. "But he's not wrong. I could likely use the help."

Nick cocked his head to the side as he considered Eric's words. He rarely heard his friend express anything that might be construed as insecurity. But he didn't ask more as Hanson returned.

"Good news. Smith is there."

"How do you know?" Nick asked, sitting up straighter.

"He's got the exact same eyes as Madame Beauchamp. There can be no mistaking him. They are moving crates into the back of the warehouse."

"What's next?" Eric asked.

"We're here to have a word with him," Nick said, starting to stand. But Hanson held up his hand.

"Are you certain the New Police should not be in attendance?"

"You're asking that now?" Nick said, raking a hand through his hair.

"Well." Hanson held up a finger. "Now that I'm here, I'm certain he's a smuggler, no question about it. He's not bringing those crates through the front, now is he? Second, he's got at least ten men with him. And third, he has broken several laws. Perhaps the police should be the ones to question him."

Nick grimaced. Hanson had several good points. "He also has a fleet of ships to escape with at the first sign of trouble."

"Still." Hanson climbed back into the carriage. "Best to proceed with caution."

"Or not," a voice called from outside the carriage. "Why don't you come on out, Your Grace? I think it's time we talked."

Smith. Nick was sure of it.

He glanced at Eric, raising a finger to his lips. Eric gave a quick jerk of his chin in understanding. "Don't let him know you're here," Nick whispered as he started for the carriage door.

Slowly, he stepped out. Both his footmen stood behind the carriage, their hands in the air. Another man held a gun on his driver.

"There's no need to threaten my staff, I only came to talk," Nick said, raising his hands.

"Did you bring me the necklace?"

"Of course not."

"And my sister? Where is she?" Smith barked.

"Safe."

"At your home? You...the duke? You call that safe?"

Nick's brows drew together. "We're childhood friends. I would never hurt her."

Smith did, in fact, have the same piercing blue eyes as Stallworth and Aubrey. They narrowed now. "Until you impregnate her and then leave her to the wolves."

He shook his head. "It isn't like that."

"How is it then?"

"I was protecting her from you."

"She's my family. She doesn't need protection from me." He waved his pistol and Nick took the smallest step back.

"If that is true, why didn't you tell her who you are?"

He saw the man's gaze waver. "We'll continue this conversation inside."

Nick's teeth ground together. Going into Smith's private domain was not going to end well. But he didn't have much of a choice.

———

AUBREY FIDGETED in the seat next to Emily. "I'm sorry this is taking so long," she whispered.

Emily shook her head. "It's all right. My maid has already told my mother I have a megrim." Emily winked.

Aubrey gave a tight nod. But the truth was, she was worried. It had now been a few hours since she'd left Nick's home and she had no idea what he might be doing. Had he seen Smith? Was he back home already?

Her father had insisted on collecting a few policemen to accompany them, but each stop made it that much longer since she'd seen Nick and she was worried.

For his safety.

For the way they'd parted. Why hadn't she told him that his words hurt because she was in love with him? Because she'd always wanted his affection to be for her. Since the age of thirteen.

She wanted his heart. That was the honest truth. And perhaps loving Nick had always been her path after all.

The carriage slowed, and the police clopping behind them drew up their horses as well.

She looked out the window to see a lone carriage sitting in the alley. Nick's carriage.

But there was no driver, nor footmen. "What the..."

Her father craned his neck, seeing the vehicle as well. "Damn," he muttered under his breath. Then he snapped the door open, exiting before the vehicle had even come to a stop.

"What are you doing?" she asked, craning her neck out the doorway as he strode toward the police.

"Saving your duke," he answered.

Nick's carriage door opened as well, and Aubrey gasped to see Eric step out of the vehicle. Handsome as ever, he had the exact same swagger.

"Eric?" she asked, lifting her skirts to climb out of the vehicle.

"By Jove, he was right. You are stunning," Eric answered with a cheeky grin.

"Surprised, are you?" she asked, some of that old hurt rising to the surface.

"Not in the least, Ducky."

While the name irritated, the words made her start. "What do you mean?"

"You were always gorgeous and I was always jealous of all the attention you lavished on him." And then he swooped down, kissing her cheek. "Since you were kind enough to bring reinforcements, I think I shall go save that egit you're going to marry."

She liked to think of him as hers but… "I'm not certain he's actually mine."

"Oh, he is. Don't you worry." Eric passed her by to join her father and the police, looking as unconcerned as if he were taking a Sunday stroll in the park.

She blinked after him. Jealous? Sincerely?

And then she followed. Because if Nick was in trouble, she was not leaving him to fend for himself. He'd done nothing but help her. It was time she returned the favor, and then it was time she told him how she really felt.

CHAPTER SEVENTEEN

Nick stared at Smith, his teeth gritting in irritation. "No."

Smith gave him a solid punch to the gut, doubling him over. "That is not the correct answer."

Pain made his legs wobble but he held himself up as he attempted to catch his breath. The question hadn't really been a question at all, so it felt fairly even to Nick. Smith had demanded his money, the necklace, and Aubrey.

Ridiculous.

"No?" he asked, knowing full well that he was inciting more violence. Sweat beaded across his forehead as his muscles clenched, waiting for the next hit. But he'd take it and several more. As many as Smith wished to dole out.

"I want the necklace and I want my sister." Smith wrapped his hand about Nick's neck and Nick grabbed the other man's arm in response, digging fingers into the tendon on the inside of his wrist.

"You can't have either," he pushed out even as Smith cut the air from his lungs.

"Big words from the man who is about to collapse to the floor."

"You mean the man who has everything you want," he answered, sinking his fist into the other man's gut.

Smith's hand jolted from his neck, the other man letting out a grunt as he doubled over. Some of the smugglers rushed closer in. He gave them all a hard glare. "He told you that you've captured a duke, didn't he?"

The men halted, their gazes growing wary as Smith straightened, pulling a pistol from his belt. "Your position doesn't frighten me." He jabbed the pistol into Nick's chest. "Your kind can all go to the devil as far as I'm concerned."

"Is that any way to speak to your future brother-in-law?" Nick knew he was playing a dangerous game, baiting the man. If Smith truly cared about Aubrey, he'd be glad to hear Nick wished to wed her. Though Nick suspected the other man didn't care a bit despite his claim of brotherly affection.

"You don't get the jewels," the other man spat. "You've got enough." Jewels? What the hell did Smith mean?

But suddenly the crack of a pistol rent the air and Nick didn't hesitate to drop to the ground as several more shots split the air, filling it with smoke.

A scream followed and he knew, without seeing, that it was Aubrey.

His heart thudded in his chest as pushed up and raced toward the sound. Through the haze of smoke he saw her, and then the wild thrumming of his pulse froze as he watched Smith grab her arm and begin dragging her away.

With a roar, he surged forward, jumping on the other man and wrapping an arm about Smith's neck. He spat in the other man's ear, "Don't you dare touch her."

"Nick," Aubrey cried as he tightened his arm.

He caught her gaze as Smith dropped to his knees. For a moment, Nick kept his arm locked. The man had tried to hurt the woman whom Nick loved.

But this was Aubrey's brother, even if he was a morally corrupt one. And so he loosened his grip. "Here!" he yelled.

A police officer rushed forward and then another, the two of them holding Smith on the ground. Nick raced to Aubrey. He stopped in front of her for just a moment before wrapping his arms about her. "What are you doing here?"

She rested her cheek on his chest, sinking into him, her voice catching as she answered. "Helping you?"

He shook his head, adjusting his grip to bring her even closer. "Sweetheart."

"I know. It was likely foolish. Foolish decisions seem to be a family trait." She looked up at him then, her hands sliding over his chest. "Like leaving your room last night. That was silly too."

The sweetest relief slid through him. "I'm sorry too. My words were the real error."

She shook her head. "None of that matters now." She lifted up on tiptoe and pressed her lips to his in a quick kiss. "Tonight we'll talk about all of it."

"Why not now?"

She looked about them. "It's a bit busy here, yet."

The police, along with Eric and Mr. Hanson, had captured several of the smugglers. "My carriage."

She shook her head. "I have to get Emily home."

"Emily's here?" he asked. "What is she doing here?"

"I didn't want to face my father alone."

He pulled her out of the warehouse and toward the carriages. "This is no place for either of you. Let's get her home." But he had to confess, he was glad she'd brought someone with her to see the marquess. "Did you learn anything from Stallworth?"

"Yes. Quite a bit."

"Tell me," he said as they reached the marquess's carriage. Emily still waited inside and Nick handed her out, taking her to his own vehicle.

Once he settled both women inside, Aubrey continued. "He tried to make Smith his heir."

Nick's jaw worked. "That's a tricky business."

Aubrey nodded. "Which is why Stallworth abandoned the endeavor. But before he did, he told Smith what he planned to do with grandmother's entire collection of jewels."

"What?" Nick asked, his chest tight with anticipation.

"Give them to me," Aubrey answered, her voice so quiet, it took him a moment to understand the words.

Emily raised a finger. "He said he wished that he'd wed Aubrey's mother and made Aubrey legitimate."

Nick scrubbed his jaw. The story matched up with what little he'd learned from Smith. Smith wished to get his hands on all the jewelry. How much was the collection worth? "My love. Are you an heiress?"

She started in surprise and then her hands clasped over her mouth. Emily let out a small yelp. "Why didn't that occur to me sooner?"

Outwardly, he smiled. He was happy for her. But inwardly, sick dread weighted his limbs. Aubrey had never been closer to the life of independence she wished for all these years.

———

AUBREY AND NICK spent the better part of the afternoon returning Emily home, making sure her mother was none the wiser, and then sending missives to both her father and Eric as well as Mr. Hanson to make sure everyone was safe at home after their adventure.

Nick left to see the police as the afternoon waned. He wanted to find out if they'd learned anything new from Smith that might affect Aubrey.

She'd stayed behind, and in the quiet, had ordered a bath to soak in and reflect on all that had happened the last few days.

She was going to be an heiress.

Had her father really willed her the jewels? She shook her head. To think she'd had the means all this time. She'd never sew another dress ever again if she chose not to.

Which made her frown.

She liked to work. Perhaps not actively waiting on customers but she enjoyed the challenges of operating a business.

But she also knew that Nick had her heart. Would being his duchess be as fulfilling as owning her shop had been?

Because between her father's and Emily's words today, she knew she'd shifted. She could live alone now, if she chose.

But with that choice now in her grasp, she had to ask herself…is that what she wished for? The answer was no.

Her life would be empty without someone to share it with. Without Nick.

She sank deeper into the water, closing her eyes.

He had a sunken tub, the luxury of it a wonder to behold and even better to soak in as she contemplated her choices.

She heard the door and her eyes popped open as she turned to see who had entered. She gasped as Nick's boots came into view. Slowly, her eyes traveled up his muscular frame, stopping where his fingers pulled at the knot in his cravat. Was he undressing?

"I'm not wearing any clothes," she said, heat filling her cheeks.

"I know," he answered as the cravat dropped to the floor, his jacket following in rapid succession. "I'm rather excited about it."

She smiled then, dipping lower in the soapy water. "But we've not talked yet and…"

"My promise stands, love. If we're not to wed, I'll not do anything that would risk your future, but we also agreed that we'd enjoy each other's company. Did we not?"

He'd saved her life, slayed her dragons, helped her reconnect with her father, and still he honored his promises. How could she ever refuse him anything?

"You heard Emily today," she said as his shirt fell away, revealing the muscular swells and valleys of his chest. "My father regrets not marrying my mother."

"Did you tell him no one regrets that more than you?"

She shook her head. "I used to regret it. I was even angry about it. And honestly, in my heart, I wanted to make others suffer for it. Eric was definitely on that list."

He pulled off his boots then and she stopped as he reached for the falls of his breeches, working the skin-tight fabric over his hips and down his legs until he stood before her without a stitch of clothing, looking for all the world like a carved statue of a god.

She drew in a sharp inhale as her gaze landed on his member, already hard and protruding from his body.

She pushed back from the rim of the tub, not frightened exactly but perhaps awed by the masculinity before her. "And me. I know you resisted my help because you were angry at me."

"I wasn't just angry. I felt like...less." She still did. A bit. He stepped into the tub, his feet only a few inches from her folded legs as he sunk into the still-hot water and then reached for her hand, slowly pulling her closer. His legs spread out on either side of her as she slid between them, her body settling into the crook of his. She let him pull her closer as she searched for the words. "You were always handsome, and titled, and rich and I was...none of those."

Her chest came into contact with his, the water adding a slickness to their skin that made her gasp in pleasure.

"You are everything that is right in this world," he whispered close to her ear. "You have enchanted me, my beautiful swan."

"Not a duck anymore?" she asked with a smile as her arms wrapped about his neck.

"You were never a duck, love. I was a fool. There is a very large difference."

Those words made her melt deeper into him. "So was I."

"What?" he asked, leaning back to look at her."

"For not taking your help sooner. For not accepting your proposal."

He stared into her eyes. "You're accepting my proposal?"

"If it still stands." She shook her head. "I have a dowry now and—"

"Those jewels are yours. As is the necklace tucked in my safe."

She smiled at that as his hands slid down her back and then skimmed over her backside, making her shiver in pleasure. "Thank you. But I have to tell you something else before we go any further."

"What is it?" he murmured as he began to trail kisses along her ear.

"It's just that..." She gasped in a breath at the tingling sensation that moved through her. "I love you."

His mouth stilled. "You love me."

She was in it now. She'd started her confession and she'd be brave enough to tell him the entirety of the truth. "It's why I didn't accept last night. I was afraid you didn't feel the same."

"After my comment about my father." He slid a hand up her back, cradling the base of her head in his large palm.

"Yes."

He let out a long breath. "I know you understand. He never showed me an ounce of affection. He barely even acknowledged my existence."

"I understand," she said and nodded, wrapping her arms tighter about his neck, her breasts sliding against his chest.

"I could say that I made the comment because I don't know how to love. No one taught me."

She dropped her forehead to his, her heart aching for him.

Still, he continued. "But the truth is, I was afraid to tell you that I loved you too."

A wave of shock traveled down her body. "You what?" She could hardly believe her ears.

Was her fairy tale actually coming true?

CHAPTER EIGHTEEN

NICK HELD her in his arms, staring into the depths of her crystal blue eyes. He loved this woman with all his heart and soul.

He couldn't deny she was a bit...reckless. But also brave, and strong, and beautiful inside and out.

He kissed her mouth, drinking her in slowly as he pressed her close. "I love you, Aubrey Fairfield. I want to marry you because, until I met you, I didn't wish for anything. Not love, or marriage. I didn't want children. I didn't even like the life I had. But somehow, thanks to you, I see everything differently now. My life is a gift that I will cherish and you...you are a treasure that I shall keep next to my heart always."

"Nick," she said in a strangled whisper. "You truly mean it? You love me too?"

How did she not know that? He'd turned his life upside down since she'd arrived. "Should I fight another villain for you? Would that prove it to you?"

She caught his gaze then, their eyes locking as their chests, pressed together, rose and fell with their heavy breaths.

He wanted her so much. Her skin slid against his, her arms around his neck, her lips moving with his as their tongues mingled together.

He pulled back once again, satisfaction rippling through him at the passion that made her gaze hazy as she panted through her swollen lips.

"So you'll marry me, love?"

"Yes," she answered, kissing him again.

He traced the curve of her ass and then dipped his hand between her legs, rumbling with appreciation as she moaned against his mouth.

"Does that mean that…" He'd not take what she didn't willingly give.

She pulled back again, looking deep into his eyes. "You want to be inside me?"

That was like asking a man if he wanted to breathe. The answer was always yes. "Would you prefer to wait until we're wed?"

She slid down his front and then pulled herself back up, their bodies sliding together as he found her nub of pleasure with his middle finger and began to stroke small circles around the bud.

"No," she said, rotating her hips to match his movements. "I don't want to wait."

That was all the encouragement he needed. Grasping her ass in both hands, he rose from the tub, water pouring down them both as her legs wrapped about his waist.

The head of his cock was already pushing into her soft folds and there was a part of him that wished to enter her standing in the bathing room.

But she'd never been with a man before and he needed to go far more slowly and carefully than that.

With that in mind, he started for the bedroom, crossing the room to set her down on the coverlet.

He settled between her thighs, his weight pressing her deeper into the blankets as she sighed out his name.

"Nick." He loved his name on her lips and he kissed her as he slid a hand up and down her length once again.

Her legs were still about his waist, which left her wide open and he slowly began to sink into her body.

He felt her tense and he stopped, looking down into her eyes. "Are you all right, my love?"

"Yes," she answered, her gaze holding his. "I'm perfect."

He continued moving slowly until he'd finally seated himself inside her. And then he kissed her until he felt her body relax against his.

Finally, he started to withdraw and then push back in.

She gasped and he stilled again. "Aubrey?"

"No." She tightened her arms. "It's good."

His rhythm was slow and soft as he began to move, aware that despite her words, it likely felt uncomfortable.

But soon her hips moved with his, her arms tight about his neck.

He kept the slow rhythm, though the tension building in him tried to push him faster. He held back, not wanting to hurt her.

But as her legs tightened about him, her heart racing against his, he knew that if he held off for a bit longer, she'd join him in his pleasure.

It was that thought that he held on to until, finally, she cried out, her insides gripping him as her finish shivered through her body.

Her undoing was his and he tossed his head back, roaring, his seed spilling as satisfaction raced through him.

And then he captured her lips with his, holding her close in his arms, their bodies still joined.

Aubrey was his past, his present, and his future.

He'd found his way forward as a duke and as a man. And he vowed, as he held her tight, to live a better life than his father before him. That was all that mattered. He'd do right by his future family and show his children the love he'd never had.

Slowly, he pulled out of her body and then lifted up to tuck them both under the covers. In his arms was where Aubrey belonged.

EPILOGUE

THE CARRIAGE RUMBLED down the rutted road, not that Aubrey noticed. She was encased in her new husband's arms, firmly settled in his lap.

How long had it been since they'd left London and their wedding breakfast? An hour? Two?

He kissed her again, his hands playing with the buttons of her dress.

"When do we stop?" she asked between kisses.

His fingers slipped over the Rivermore Diamond that circled her neck. "Hours from now."

"Hours?" They were on their way to his home in Bath for their honeymoon. "We don't get to be together for hours?"

He gave her a sly grin, his hand sliding down her leg and then up under her skirt. "What shall we do until then?"

She gave a small giggle, her body already heating with excitement. "I can't believe we're actually married."

His hand slowed. "I can, love. This is exactly where I was meant to be."

She traced his cheek with one of her fingers. Some part of her still couldn't believe that he wanted her for his duchess. She didn't say it out loud but he clearly saw the feeling etched on her features.

"Aubrey," he murmured, his fingers coming to the shell of her ear and tracing their curve until he came to the blue diamonds attached to her ears. A gift from her father. The stones that matched the necklace he'd given to her at her birth. An advancement on her inheritance.

"Yes?" she asked, holding her breath as she waited to hear what he had to say.

He began to methodically remove her gloves, revealing a fourth blue diamond, not part of the set but an engagement gift from Nick. It winked in the dim light. He'd promised her that the jewels were her insurance policy. A way to ensure that she never went without again.

"You know better than that."

She did. "It's not you. I couldn't ask for any more. I sometimes still feel like the girl in the village that no one wanted."

"Not true. Eric was clear that he always thought you a great beauty."

That made her smile. Eric had not attended their wedding because he'd left London to meet his prospective bride. But she'd wished he'd been there. "I'll have to thank him for sharing that."

"Perhaps you'll get a chance at his nuptials."

She smiled. "I'd like that very much."

"You won't be too busy then, managing your dress shops?"

She shook her head. Another way that Nick had ensured her future, no matter what came their way...he'd purchased her original shop and another in Bath. Another seamstress would work for her, but she'd have her own businesses to sustain herself should she ever need it. "I think I can make time for Eric."

"And your husband? Will you have time for him too?"

"Always," she whispered, kissing him again. Nick was her happily ever after.

The Earl who Escaped

All That Glitters

.   .   .

Tammy Andresen

THE EARL WHO ESCAPED

TAMMY ANDRESEN

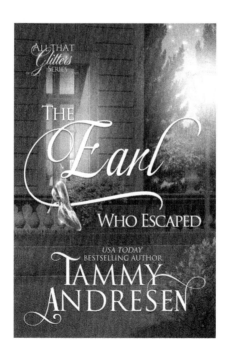

Lady Ella Cartwright stood dutifully at the bottom of the stairs next to her sister, Fern, her hands demurely folded. Outwardly she was the picture of calm and serene compliance. But inwardly, she waged war, a tumult of emotions seething beneath her calm exterior.

She had two distinct periods in her life: before and after. In the period before, her family had made a trip to the ocean, one of the happiest memories of her life. She remembered her parents lounging in the sand, talking quietly as her and her sister played. Ella had waded into the water and then, after a fashion, she'd ducked her head under the water. On the surface, all appeared calm and tranquil, but underneath, the water teamed with life and activity. That was Ella.

But Ella snapped back to the present as their stepmother gave them both a narrow-eyed glare, her knowing gaze attempting to find the chink in Ella's armor but Ella gave nothing away.

"Hmmm," her stepmother said. Lady Vivian Sanbridge was no fool. She surely saw through Ella's charade.

They both knew the truth…Ella's compliance was a fraud and her stepmother only pretended to care about her stepdaughters. But neither could outwardly accuse the other.

"Tell them, Mother…" her stepsister Melisandre huffed from behind her mother, her arms crossed and her bottom lip stuck out. "Tell them that I know I left the ivory-handled brush on my dressing table and now it's gone."

"Hush," her stepmother soothed automatically, her gaze never leaving Ella's.

Ella posed her features into a sympathetic mask. "Are you certain? Perhaps it fell?"

"I checked everywhere." Melisandre pointed an accusing finger over her mother's shoulder, her brown eyes growing hard and angry.

"Your dressing room?" Ella asked in a false attempt to appear helpful. Melisandre's dressing room was, in fact, Ella's childhood bedroom. Ella had been moved to a tiny back bedroom, in order to make way for Melisandre's mountain of dresses, shoes, and jewelry.

Melisandre huffed. "Of course I checked my dressing room." Her lip curled into a sneer. "We all know you took it, Ella. Why you insist on denying it is beyond me. Why don't you just admit it and take your punishment?"

She had no intention of saying any such thing. Nor did she plan to be punished. "Sister, dear, why would you say such things about me?"

Fern looked at the ceiling knowing full well that Ella had absolutely taken the brush. She and Fern each had their subtle ways they enacted punishment over their stepsister. Thieving happened to be Ella's. Fern was far more direct.

Melisandre threw up her hands, her much larger arms and embellished sleeves looking like wings behind their stepmother. It wasn't that Melisandre was large. She was likely perfectly sized, it was more that Ella and Fern weren't well fed. They were both small by comparison.

"I say those things about you because they are true. You're a horrible, no good, dastardly—"

"What's that?" her and Fern's father called from the top of the stairs and all four women turned to meet his gaze, Melisandre falling silent.

Ella kept her perfected veneer solidly in place. She'd learned long ago that her father was not an ally in this quiet war being waged under his roof. At first, he appeared sympathetic enough, hugging her even as he told her to get along with their new family. That blending the two together would take time.

But he seemed to turn a blind eye to her and Fern's inferior clothing, their lack of food, their simple rooms, and the fact they had almost no lessons. After nearly a decade of living under her stepmother's rule, Ella had learned to fight back subtly and with plausible deniability. A lesson Melisandre had never learned. She didn't have to. "She's accused me of stealing her brush, Papa. As though I don't have my own."

"Of course you do," her father answered, coming down the stairs. "It was a present I gave you last year for your birthday."

"Exactly," she gave her father a bright smile. "Which makes it more precious than any jeweled piece."

"It wasn't jeweled," Melisandre pouted. "It was ivory."

"Oh, of course. I must have forgotten what it looked like," she lied, knowing full well that the brush was tucked under a loose floorboard beneath her bed.

Her stepmother's lip curled into what could only be described as a sneer. "If Ella says she did not take it than she did not."

Her stepmother, on the other hand, knew how to play her part well with her husband. She told him all the things he wished to hear, and then did exactly as she wanted, Ella's father seeming none the wiser.

The other woman absolutely thought that Ella had taken it and she'd do her utmost to prove her theory. But the countess would do so quietly....

How did he not notice that all of the pin money went to Melisandre? Or that Melisandre received all the new dresses? All the lessons?

"Of course, my sweet Ella didn't take your things, Melisandre. We're a family after all," he smiled at his two daughters, Fern giving him a glare back. If Ella played the game, Fern froze everyone out with stoic silence and icy glares.

Her father didn't respond however, as his eyes rounded and his shoulders hunched, wracking coughs seizing his lungs.

Ella truly winced then. There was no acting. Despite everything, she loved her father and besides...what would life be like without him? Would her stepmother toss them out? Marry them off to some toads?

Ella stepped closer, her arm wrapping about her father's shoulders as he gasped for breath. "Relax," she whispered. "Try to breathe."

"My Ella," he said between coughs, his head coming to her shoulder. "My sweet Ella."

Melisandre snorted, a sound Ella pointedly ignored. When her father had recovered, he straightened, looking at his wife, the disagreement over the brush already forgotten. "When does Lord Pembroke arrive?"

"Soon. No later than a fortnight," she answered, placing a hand on his arm. They all knew the truth. Her father was dying. It was only a matter of time.

One might think that her stepmother's light touch on her father's arm meant that she cared, but Ella knew the truth. All her sneaking had earned her loads of valuable information over the years but none better than what she'd acquired two nights' prior. Her stepmother had a plot. She was going to attempt to marry Melisandre to the new Earl of Sanbridge, her father's heir.

He was some distant cousin that was already a viscount. Lord Pembroke. Ella didn't recall ever meeting him; if she had, it was when she was very small before her mother passed away.

Ella gave her first real smile of the morning. She had a plan as well. And it was her best yet. She wasn't just going to steal a silly brush, or even a dress that she reworked into her own. No.

She was going to pull off the biggest heist of her life. She planned to steal Melisandre's groom. And it was going to be magnificent.

———

Lord Eric Henderson, Viscount Pembroke, yawned as his carriage rumbled along a country road toward nowhere England.

He jested. The place had a name and he knew it too...it was to be his home after all. But his head pounded from all the ale he'd drank at the inn the night before and his thoughts were covered in a hangover haze.

He scrubbed his face, wishing he had some snacks, and a large cup of water, and perhaps, another ale.

He sniffed the air noting that something smelled rather stale, but as he pushed into a more upright position, he realized that the smell was wafting off his own clothes.

Though a viscount, Eric had never been much for propriety, and he stayed as far away from polite society as he could. He scratched at his stubbly chin, smacking his lips to clear away the paste in his mouth.

The sun was casting a soft light in the sky, the sort that meant it was either sun up or sun down, but he had no idea which. Had he slept the day away or awoken after only a few hours of drunken sleep? He couldn't say.

"Driver," he called, thumping the head of his cane against the wall. "Where are we?"

"Essex," the driver called back.

"Where are we going again?"

"Essex," the man said again, having the decency not to laugh.

"Shit," he murmured, sitting up straighter in his seat. "How long until we arrive?"

"Minutes? An hour?" the man said.

"Will we pass through any villages?" he desperately needed a bath. Despite his devil-may-care attitude, not even he would arrive in this state as a guest. He knew he didn't deserve their hospitality, but his hosts didn't need to be apprised of his unworthiness. At least not within the first minute of his arrival.

"Did already, my lord. Should I try to turn the carriage?"

Eric let out a soft groan as he flicked open the curtain. Turning the carriage took space and could be tricky depending on the road. But in the last rays of the sun, he noted a river up ahead. "No need, just pull over."

He'd not be able to shave, nor could he completely change but he could freshen up at least.

With that in mind, he had the driver pull onto the side of the rutted country lane and then he stepped from the carriage, making his way down the steep bank, his Hessians sliding in the dirt. It was nearly summer but a stiff breeze still chilled his skin as he stripped off his waistcoat, vest, cravat, and shirt. His footman tossed him a cake of soap and then, kneeling down, he plunged his head and neck into the freezing water. It cleared a great deal of fog from his thoughts and as his head emerged, he began to scrub.

He briefly considered stripping off the rest of his clothes but the road was open, and in the distance, a large estate rose up into the twilight. He debated for a moment as he started up at the stately mansion.

Was that to be his new home? He belonged there even less than he did Pembroke, his ancestral seat. The thought of Pembroke made him grimace and he scrubbed harder.

He could hear the footman taking down his trunk from its spot on the back of the carriage, undoing the latches. "Reeves, I've changed my mind, I'll take a new set of breeches as well. These one might walk away on me if I wear them any longer."

He may as well make a decent impression. He wasn't just coming here to meet the earl who was a distant family member and whose earldom Eric would inherit, he was coming here to meet a bride.

He grimaced at the idea. Him. Married. It suited him even less than sobriety or society events. But he wasn't certain he had a choice. Well, he always had a choice. But this earldom had thousands of people who depended upon it and his distant cousin, the current earl, had suggested that his stepdaughter would be most suited to aiding him in the management of such holdings. Considering he'd still be responsible for his viscountcy, it wasn't a bad idea provided the woman understood his parameters. This was no love match and he was never going to be the doting husband. He'd keep his activities discreet and that was about the most he'd promise.

All straight in his mind, he kicked off his boots and waded into the water, still in his breeches. He'd give them a wash on his body and then he'd kick them off, scrubbing quickly before Reeves delivered him fresh clothing.

His stomach grumbled, likely complaining that after all that ale, he'd not eaten a bite to eat but he ignored it, scrubbing at the material until, satisfied, he started to unbutton the falls.

"Oh my," a feminine voice called. He instantly stood up straight, one hand holding the pants together as he scanned both riverbanks.

And that's when he saw her laying in the grass. She was propped on one elbow, her golden hair shimmering in the dying sun. Her body sloped to a narrow waist even as her hip flared creating the most enticing feminine line. "I beg your pardon, madame. I did not—"

"It's quite all right, Lord Pembroke," she called back before rising from her spot and moving toward him.

Her body swayed with such fluid grace that he was mesmerized for a moment, long enough that she'd nearly reached him before he realized that she held a pasty in each of her hands. "How do you know who I am?"

That's when his gaze rose to her face and every muscle in his body clenched. Even in the dark, he could make out the clear blue of her eyes, her adorable little upturned nose, her sweet, full mouth. She looked like an angel. "I make it my business to know most things that happen at Castledon. And your visit is much anticipated." Her words rang of something devilish despite her appearance, and he found his brows rising even as he assessed her from his position down in the water with her above. He was still shirtless, not that he cared, but he watched as her gaze took him in.

Despite being a terrible drunkard, he still found time to box and ride, finding physical activity was the only other outlet to the ceaseless turning of his thoughts, so he knew she'd noted all of his muscles. "And who are you to make such things your business?"

She was a picture of contradictions. Her accent was fine but her dress simple and rather worn looking. Her face had all the grace of a lady but she was slender like a servant who worked hard and didn't have access to proper food.

"No one of consequence," she answered with a wave her hand, the delicate pasty still resting in her palm. "At least not anymore."

"No one of consequence?" he asked, with a furrow of his brow. "That's no answer at all."

"Hungry?" she asked, sitting once again in the grass as she gave him a smile. "I brought an extra."

He was famished and his stomach gave a decided gurgle at her offer and the sight of food. "Your name, madame?" He narrowed his gaze, determined to feel as though he had some purchase in this conversation.

"Lady Ella," she answered with a sigh.

"Lady Ella?" he asked moving toward her, one hand still holding his falls together.

"Eldest daughter of the Earl of Sanbridge."

"Oh," he said even as he worked his way up the steep wet ground toward her. "I see."

Keep up with all the latest news, sales, freebies, and releases by joining my newsletter!

www.tammyandresen.com

Hugs!

ABOUT THE AUTHOR

Tammy Andresen lives with her husband and three children just outside of Boston, Massachusetts. She grew up on the Seacoast of Maine, where she spent countless days dreaming up stories in blueberry fields and among the scrub pines that line the coast. Her mother loved to spin a yarn and Tammy filled many hours listening to her mother retell the classics. It was inevitable that at the age of eighteen, she headed off to Simmons College, where she studied English literature and education. She never left Massachusetts but some of her heart still resides in Maine and her family visits often.

Find out more about Tammy:
http://www.tammyandresen.com/
https://www.facebook.com/authortammyandresen
https://twitter.com/TammyAndresen
https://www.pinterest.com/tammy_andresen/
https://plus.google.com/+TammyAndresen/

OTHER TITLES BY TAMMY

Lords of Scandal

Duke of Daring

Marquess of Malice

Earl of Exile

Viscount of Vice

Baron of Bad

Earl of Sin

——————————

Earl of Gold

Earl of Baxter

Duke of Decandence

Marquess of Menace

Duke of Dishonor

Baron of Blasphemy

Viscount of Vanity

Earl of Infamy

Laird of Longing

——————————

Duke of Chance

Marquess of Diamonds

Queen of Hearts

Baron of Clubs

Earl of Spades

King of Thieves

Marquess of Fortune

Too Wicked to Want

How to Reform a Rake
Don't Tell a Duke You Love Him
Meddle in a Marquess's Affairs
Never Trust an Errant Earl
Never Kiss an Earl at Midnight
Make a Viscount Beg

Wicked Lords of London
Earl of Sussex
My Duke's Seduction
My Duke's Deception
My Earl's Entrapment
My Duke's Desire
My Wicked Earl

Brethren of Stone
The Duke's Scottish Lass
Scottish Devil
Wicked Laird
Kilted Sin
Rogue Scot
The Fate of a Highland Rake

A Laird to Love
Christmastide with my Captain
My Enemy, My Earl
Heart of a Highlander
A Scot's Surrender
A Laird's Seduction

Taming the Duke's Heart

Taming a Duke's Reckless Heart

Taming a Duke's Wild Rose

Taming a Laird's Wild Lady

Taming a Rake into a Lord

Taming a Savage Gentleman

Taming a Rogue Earl

Fairfield Fairy Tales

Stealing a Lady's Heart

Hunting for a Lady's Heart

Entrapping a Lord's Love: Coming in February of 2018

American Historical Romance

Lily in Bloom

Midnight Magic

The Golden Rules of Love

Boxsets!!

Taming the Duke's Heart Books 1-3

American Brides

A Laird to Love

Wicked Lords of London

Printed in Great Britain
by Amazon

18545858R00088